I0544000

Scorned In Darkness

Scorned in Blood Trilogy, Volume 2

Ana DiPinto

Published by Ana DiPinto, 2022.

SCORNED IN DARKNESS

First edition. September 7, 2022.

Copyright © 2022 Ana DiPinto.

ISBN: 978-1736141229

Written by Ana DiPinto.

Table of Contents

One 1

Two 9

Three 15

Four 19

Five 27

Six 35

Seven 43

Eight 51

Nine 57

Ten 63

Eleven 69

Twelve 77

Thirteen 83

Fourteen 89

Fifteen 97

Sixteen 103

Seventeen 109

Eighteen 117

Nineteen 125

Twenty 133

Twenty-One 143

Twenty-Two 149

Twenty-Three 157

Twenty-Four 163

Twenty-Five 171

Twenty-Six 179

Twenty-Seven 187

Twenty-Eight 195

Twenty-Nine 203

Thirty 211

Thirty-One 219

To Crazy movie night with my Dad

One

"Are you ready?" A heavy, accented voice came from the doorway. Jace turned around to see his oldest friend and business partner Alan standing at the entrance to his room. Alan tugged at the collar of his suit as he cleared his throat. Jace straightened his tie and grabbed his black suit jacket from his bed.

"Never ready for this. Let's just get it over with."

Outside, the temperature was warming up as spring was turning into summer. The clear blue sky was bright, and the sun reflected off the sidewalk. A pretty day for such a sad occasion. Jace put his hand to his forehead to block the sunlight from his eyes. He settled into the passenger seat of Alan's car and rested his elbow on the door as they drove away.

Moments later, they pulled into the parking lot of the funeral home. Jace stepped somberly out of the car. The air outside smelled of fresh tar and recently cut grass. He pulled on his suit jacket and adjusted his tie one last time as he crossed the pavement. His hand rested on the door for a minute before he managed to walk through it. Alan put a hand on his shoulder to offer him comfort, but all Jace wanted was not to have to be here. He wanted not to feel the aching pain twisting in the pit of his stomach. He wanted his fiancée Cloe to be alive and at home beside him. Instead, she was lying dead in the casket at the other end of the room.

Mourners offered their condolences and signed the guest book as they filed in. Friends, family, and co-workers, all acquaintances of Cloe, chatted with each other sharing their memories. The sounds of their voices filled the room, but Jace could hardly hear them. The floral pattern on the wallpaper began to swirl. Jace's hands began to shake, and his palms grew clammy. He spotted a chair in the corner and sat down, resting his head in his hands.

"You, ok?" Alan stood over Jace, holding out a cup of water for him.

Jace silently shook his head. He refused the water and instead pulled out a flask from his inside jacket pocket. He twisted off the cap and took a sip of the whiskey inside.

"Man, you need to drink something other than liquor. And when was the last time you ate something?" Alan was still holding onto the clear plastic cup. His 6-foot frame cast a shadow over his grieving friend. The concern on his face was palpable.

Jace shrugged in response to his friend's question. He knew Alan was looking out for him, but Alan didn't understand. No one understood. Jace was the reason Cloe was dead. He had to live with that. He couldn't live with it.

"Come on. The service is about to start." Alan turned towards the other room, where everyone had gathered for the wake. He offered a hand to Jace though Jace brushed him aside.

Jace rose to his feet and followed Alan across the funeral home. Wooden chairs were set in rows across the room. Large bouquets of flowers had been placed in every corner and at each end of the casket. A collage of photos was set on an easel next to the podium where the eulogy would be given.

Jace stared at his fiancée, lying lifeless in the white casket. Her head rested on a pink silk pillow. She looked peaceful, but she didn't look like herself, Jace thought. She would never have worn such heavy makeup. Why did they use red lipstick? She didn't wear colors like that. Even the curls in her hair appeared different; they did not look natural. And what was with the dress she was wearing? It was long, made of lace and chiffon with a beaded neckline, and it was purple. Cloe would never wear clothing that color. And who dressed her up so formally?

Cloe wasn't a formal person. Sure, she dressed up for work, but she was a jeans and t-shirt kind of girl. She wouldn't want to spend eternity in a fancy party dress. This was all wrong.

Cloe's mother was the first person to get up and speak. She stood up at the podium. Her cheeks were flushed red, and her eyes were puffy from crying. Jace listened to her choking back her tears as she spoke while he sat there, choking back tears of his own. He didn't know the next few people who followed her, and he was sure whatever they had to say was nice. He didn't hear them, however, as his mind drifted off into his own memories. The noises around him were drowning out, and the world around him faded away as he descended into his own private thoughts.

CLOE SAT AT THE KITCHEN table, her notebook open and pen in hand. The laptop sat open in front of her as she jotted her notes down. Jace stood against the wall, watching her. Her hair was pulled back in a half ponytail and a few loose curls dangled in front of her face. The glasses she rarely wore were perched on the bridge of her nose. She was so immersed in her work that she didn't notice him standing there.

"Hey, beautiful. What you doing?" He had finally said to her. She glanced up at him and smiled. Her face lit up bright and happy. He smiled back.

"Searching venues." She replied.

"For our wedding?" He asked.

"Of course." Her smile widened. "You want to see what I found so far? You can help me narrow it down."

"Yea. But you don't just want to use your hotel?" Cloe was the event planner for one of the hotels in town. Jace had just assumed they'd have the wedding there or at least the reception. But he'd have been happy with wherever she chose.

"That's an option, probably the cheapest too." She laughed. "But I thought we could look into some other places too."

"Whatever you want. Let's see what you got there." Jace sat down next to Cloe, and together they looked over the wedding venues she had pulled up on her computer screen.

A COLD HAND RESTED on Jace's shoulder, shaking him from his memories. He shuttered at the chill that ran down his spine and turned his head around. The room sat dark and empty. No one stood behind him. All the guests had gone. Silence filled the air. A flicker of movement crossed the room, a shadow in the dark—a vampire.

Jace lept from his seat. He ran to the front door of the funeral home and peered outside into the empty parking lot. When had it gotten dark? How long had he been sitting in that same spot? Time seemed to stand still as the hours had passed without him noticing. Something else tapped his shoulder, another hand. It was warmer this time, Human.

"What just happened?" Alan's voice asked from behind him. The look on his face was puzzled and concerned.

"Nothing?" Jace closed the door stepping back inside the funeral home. There was no way he could explain to Alan what had just occurred and who it was he was looking for when he ran to the door. He pushed past his friend though Alan stayed close to his side.

"Maybe we should go. Come on, let's get out of here, maybe get you some food."

"No. You go. I want to stay a little longer. I'll call a ride share in a little bit."

"You sure, man? I'm getting a little worried about you."

"Yea, I'm sure. I'll be fine."

"Ok, but make sure you eat something."

"I will."

Alan left without pressing the issue any further. Jace stood alone now in the empty funeral home. He flipped through the pages of the guest book, glancing at the names of everyone who'd signed it. Cloe had so many friends. So many had cared for her and would now miss her. A tear fell from the corner of his eye and landed on the open pages. He tapped the spot dry doing his best not to smear the ink of the name written there. It only blurred a little. Jace closed the book and went back into the room where Cloe lay in her casket.

He walked the perimeter of the room. The smell of fresh flowers, antiseptic, and something else surrounded him. Death, that's what he smelled, the faint stench of death.

He stepped over to the casket. He had avoided getting too close all day, but now here he was looking down at Cloe. Her hands folded across her chest. He reached down and placed a hand atop of hers. Her skin was soft and cold—cold like the vampires. But Cloe wouldn't be coming back from the dead like his old friend Harper had done.

Harper had turned up last winter after three years of no one knowing what had happened to her. For three years, everyone thought her boyfriend Zaine had killed her. Maybe there was a bit of truth to that because if Zaine hadn't almost killed her in the first place, then the vampire wouldn't have gotten to her. And then Harper wouldn't have come back from the dead seeking Jace's help. Jace would still be living blissfully ignorant of any vampire existence, and Cloe would still be alive. But no, Harper had become a vampire, and Jace had agreed to help her, and now Cloe was dead as a result of that.

"I'm so sorry," Jace whispered to Cloe's corpse. "I'll see you get the justice you deserve."

As he turned to leave the room, a woman stood in the doorway. Her familiar copper hair fell in waves past her shoulders. The simple black dress she wore was belted at the waist and stopped just above the knee. Her signature combat boots were on her feet. As she stepped into the room, Jace felt a sudden wave of relief. If anyone could help him get justice for Cloe, it would be Sarah Higgins.

"Hi, Jace. I'm so sorry for your loss," Sarah said as she reached out with a comforting touch to his forearm.

"Thank you, Sarah. I'm glad you came," Jace replied.

"Sorry I missed the wake. I just finished closing up the shop for the night and came right here."

"It's ok. I'm glad you're here now. It will give us a chance to talk in private."

"What's going on?" Sarah asked.

"I know we've told everyone that Cloe died from an illness, but that's not what happened."

"What was it?"

"Suicide. Well, sort of. I don't think she did it on her own." Jace lowered his voice as he spoke.

"What do you mean?" Sarah furrowed her brow. Her head made a slight tilt as she stared at Jace.

"I think they were in her head. I think they made her do it." Jace glanced around the room as if he were checking to ensure there was no one around to hear him.

"Who? Jace, you're not making any sense."

"Vampires."

Jace walked Sarah over to the casket. He pushed aside Cloe's hair. Her curls had been sprayed with so much hairspray they felt harsh against his skin. He grimaced at how they had ruined her. Cloe's curls had always been natural and soft. He showed Sarah the puncture wounds on her neck just below her hairline. Sarah let out a small gasp.

"You know she had been sick, and I suspected vampires had something to do with it. It was so sudden, and the symptoms so similar to how I had felt when Harper had bitten me. Although her symptoms, as you know, were much more severe. It was clear to me that whoever was doing this to her was taking way more blood than Harper had taken from me. I checked her a few times while she was still in the hospital, but I had never found anything. You see, whoever did this hid it well," Jace explained. He fixed Cloe's hair in place back over her shoulder.

"I see."

"That day I came to your shop to get some things to place around her apartment, that's when I found her. She had been home from the hospital a few days and seemed to be getting better. When I got to her house, I heard the bathwater running. I thought nothing of it at first. I put up everything in the living room. Then as I went to take care of her room, I walked past the bathroom, and that's when I saw all the water on the floor. I banged on the door, and when Cloe didn't answer, I rushed in. She was lying there in the tub. The water spilling over the tub onto the floor was full of blood. She had cut her wrists open. I pulled her from the tub, but it was too late. She was already gone before I had gotten there. That's when I finally saw the wounds on her neck." More tears began to fill Jace's eyes, and he blinked them away.

"Oh my god, Jace. I had no idea," Sarah said as she brought her hand up to her mouth.

"Yea, her mother and I decided it was best if we just told everyone it was the illness that killed her. Some of her family is very religious."

"I understand."

"So, you see, Sarah, this is my fault. I brought the vampires into our lives. I have to make it right for her."

"Don't say that, Jace. You can't blame yourself. This isn't your fault."

"But it is. If I hadn't agreed to help Harper, none of this would have happened. I should never have gone to that house. If I would have just stayed away, Cloe would still be alive instead of lying dead in that box. So, will you help me, Sarah? Will you help me get justice for Cloe?"

"Jace, you have to stop this. This is not your fault. You wouldn't have been able to refuse Harper even if you wanted to. If she wanted your help that bad, there would have been nothing you could have done. She'd had forced you one way or another. Once she bit you, you were under her control whether you realized it or not." Sarah's words were less than comforting, but Jace knew she meant well.

"But will you help me? Either way, I'm going to find the vampire that did this to her. With or without you. But I'd rather have your help."

"And then what are you going to do? What will you do when you find this vampire?"

"I will destroy them."

Sarah placed her hand on Jace's arm. She glanced over at Cloe, lying in the casket, and then looked back at Jace. "I will help you."

Two

S he watched as the blood spilled from her arm to the floor. Each drop turning from red to black. The silver of the blade in her opposite hand touched her freshly cut flesh. It burned her skin, but this is what she deserved. The blade had been dipped in the oils that were supposed to be harmful to her kind. But Luca had survived a stab from this same dagger, and so would she. She removed the dagger and watched as the wounds healed themselves. Then repeated the process.

"Harper! I thought you were dead!" Chloe's words echoed in her memories.

Another cut across her wrist.

"What's going on?" Cloe had asked.

She swiped the blade again.

"Wait, Harper! What are you doing? Wait! Harper, stop!" Over and over again, the screams of her best friend echoed in her ears and the images replayed in her mind.

Harper held her right hand in front of her, the dagger in the other. She raised the dagger over her shoulder, bringing it swiftly back down through the palm of her hand. She clenched her jaw. Blood splattered from the fresh wound. The full length of the blade stuck through her palm. Her skin stained dark red. She squeezed her eyes shut tight. Sucking in a breath of air through her clenched teeth, she pulled the dagger out of her hand.

She looked down at the hole in her hand. That wound would take a few days to heal, unlike the minor slashes she had previously made in her wrist, which healed in mere minutes. She opened her armoire and tore a strip of fabric from one of her cotton shirts. Then she wrapped the cloth around the gaping wound in her hand. Blood soaked through the layers of material, so she tore another strip, wrapping, and wrapping until the blood stopped.

The room began to spin. Her mouth became dry, and her throat grew numb. She gasped for water like a human. She could feel the poison of the oils flowing throw her, burning her from the inside, but she resisted any urges to call for help. This would pass, she knew. Instead, she laid down on her bed, staring at the ceiling while she waited for the effects to wear off.

Harper crept out of the large house she shared with the other vampires; Dac, Nikolai, Quentin, and Emmaline. It was not hard to go unnoticed these days now that everyone's attention was elsewhere.

Last winter Harper had found herself mixed up in a long-time feud between Dac, Nikolai, and some older vampires. One of those vampires was Dac's brother Luca, and the others were Nikolai's wife Una and son Alex. All of whom everyone thought were dead.

Harper found out that she was somehow a descendant of Una's, and that was the reason she bore such a striking resemblance to her. Luca, Una, and Alex had used that to lure Nikolai to Noxwood. They had kidnapped Harper and kept her in a room similar to the one Una had been held in centuries before when she had been taken by Luca. Harper remembered the anger in Alex's voice as he told the story of how Una had survived her own vampire attack and how he had grown up without his parents. They had both blamed Nikolai for not saving Una and spent centuries searching for him to get their revenge. She remembered the look on Nikolai's face when he realized Una was alive and this man he had never known, Alex, was his son.

She shivered at the memory of the cold look on Una's face as she stabbed Nikolai in the back. A tear dripped from Harper's eye as she recalled Una's sword sticking out of Nikolai's torso. The blood dripped off the edge of the sword. Harper was chained to the wall. Quentin was there. He was fighting Alex. Nikolai fell to the ground. Dac had come in at that moment and dragged Nikolai away. The rest of the night was a blur.

Someone had unchained her and carried her away. Maybe it was Quentin, but she couldn't be sure. By that time, she had gone nearly unconscious from the lack of sustenance. The next thing Harper remembered was being back here in Aura City. Quentin and Emmaline were at the house caring for Nikolai. They spent every waking hour at his side, never leaving him alone. Dac had stayed behind in Noxwood.

AS HARPER WALKED THROUGH the streets of Aura city, her stomach turned, thinking of all that happened just a few months ago but also of what she was about to do. The night air was warm. The sky was clear. It should have been a beautiful night, but it wasn't. Nothing was beautiful in Harper's eyes anymore. Everything had changed after last winter. More importantly, she had changed.

She no longer had to blend in now that she knew how to go about being unseen by humans. She'd always thought it was so easy for Quentin because although he was a vampire, he had never been human. But she had since learned it was more of an illusion, a controlling of the mind rather than the actual act of turning oneself invisible. The same way she learned last fall that she could control the weather with her mind, she could also influence how people saw her and if they saw her. The more crowded the area, the harder it was to completely conceal her appearance, so she kept to the shadows.

The crowds of people that still walked the streets rushed past her, unaware of her presence. She waited patiently in the dark cover of the alleyway between the tall gothic church and the row of townhouses. Soon enough, the stream of people will have withered down to a few lonely stragglers. And that's when she would make her move.

A couple walked past. They held hands and laughed out loud at each other's jokes. They reminded Harper of her and Zaine when they had first gotten together. She almost smiled in spite of herself when she thought of those first days. She and Zaine would walk on the boardwalk or sit on the beach in Aura Springs, where she lived back then. Sometimes they would talk for hours, and others, they would enjoy each other's company in comfortable silence. Some nights they would just stay in and watch movies either at her apartment or at his. It never mattered as long as they were together.

But then, something had changed. He had changed. He'd become angry and controlling. She searched her brain; wondering had there been signs of it before. Had he always been that way, and somehow, she just missed it. Was that how Luca or Alex or whoever it was had been so successful in manipulating him? Or was it just because they were vampires, and he was human? No. She had seen the way Zaine had treated his next girlfriend. It was the same way he had treated her right before he killed her. But was that Harper's fault? She had been tormenting his dreams when she was going after revenge. The anger seethed inside her when she thought about it. The guilt plagued her. And when she looked at who was to blame, it was all of them. Luca, Alex, Una, Zaine and even Nikolai. They were all to blame for what she had become and for what she was going to do now.

The earlier crowded street was now quiet and almost empty. A pile of black trash bags sat on the curb across the street. The smell of summer, of heat, rats, garbage, and human blood surrounded her senses. Her moment was here. A man passed by the alleyway. The blue light of his cell phone screen illuminated his face. He kept a steady pace, face down, looking into his phone. Harper pounced from her hiding place. She grabbed the man. One arm around his waist while her other hand covered the man's mouth. He kicked and struggled to free himself as she dragged him into the alleyway. The man's cell phone dropped to the ground. The screen shattered and went dark. His muffled screams were too low to be heard. Harper opened her mouth and dug her sharp fangs into his neck. The blood poured from the man's vein down Harper's throat. The essence of life filled her spirit as the blood-filled her thirst.

She hadn't experienced this taking of life in her first few years as a vampire. Dac and Nikolai had forbidden it. They taught her to suppress her vampiric instincts, to be ashamed of them. But then she tasted the pleasures of taking blood from the human body. The first time was when she sought information from Zaine by feasting on his blood, though she hadn't been the one actually to kill him. The second time was when Luca tricked her into thinking the victim was already dead. Except he wasn't, and it was an experience like no other. It was more than feeding on blood from the donations they received at the house – that was quenching a hunger. But this, this was like feeding life back into her very soul.

HARPER SNUCK BACK INTO the house through the back door that led into the kitchen. It was dark just as Harper had expected. This had become typical after their return from Noxwood, since then everything had changed. With Dac gone and Nikolai injured, they no longer had their formal feedings every night in the grand dining room. All the common rooms remained unused and dark. Quentin stayed vigilant over Nikolai's bedside throughout the night until he retired to his room at daybreak. Emmaline stayed in her own room unless retrieving blood for herself or Quentin to drink or to refill Nikolai's supply. If Quentin needed the leave the house, Emmaline would take over watch of Nikolai. It was eerily quiet every night now. The house remained lifeless.

Harper moved through the darkened kitchen to the bathroom down the hall. She turned the knobs on the sink. The clear water fell from the faucet like a waterfall. She cupped the water in both of her hands, bringing it to her mouth, rinsing the blood from her fangs. She spit the water into the sink. The now bloody water swirled in a red spiral down the drain. She wiped her mouth with her arm and went to check on Nikolai.

She stood in the doorway of Nikolai's room. A single lamp in the corner dimly lit the room. Nikolai laid motionless. His skin was so pale it was almost entirely transparent. The IV in his arm pumped the blood into his veins. Harper could see it travel through him, feeding his body.

"How is he?" She asked Quentin, who was just changing the bag of blood.

"No change," he answered, barely glancing at her.

"Shouldn't he be healing by now, though? It's been months."

"It will take some time. How long, I don't know. The blade punctured his heart when Una stabbed him. The heart takes the longest to heal. Plus, we don't know how much, if any, poison was on that blade. It could be a few more months or even years before he opens his eyes, and even then, it may still be longer before he is completely healed."

"But I don't understand. Luca recovered from his attack and...." Harper trailed off before finishing her statement.

"Yes, but we don't know how that recovery was," Quentin replied. "What happened to your hand?" He asked, noticing the thick white cloth wrapped around Harper's right hand.

Harper looked down at her hand, then tucked it behind her back. "Nothing," she said.

"I hope you're not keeping secrets again. Remember your actions have consequences." Quentin looked over at Nikolai, sounding as though he was about to break into a lecture. To Harper's relief, he didn't.

"I'm not. I promise it's nothing." She hoped she sounded convincing enough as she turned and walked out of the room. *Great, now he'll be watching me again*, she thought to herself.

Three

The cellar was dark and cool despite the warming weather outside. Condensation dripped from the concrete walls. The rat in the corner sat staring at Dac with its nocturnal eyes. Dac sat in his chair staring back, sucking the humid air of the cellar into his undead lungs. He could barely remember the last time he had left this room, but he didn't care. The cellar had become his tomb, and he was content with living the rest of his days in eternal darkness. Confinement was all he deserved. He would stay here until he finally withered into eternal sleep.

"There he is, my brother, self-loathing as always," Luca descended down the steps. The sound of his voice broke Dac from his isolated stare. The red glow of his eyes flickered like the burning flames of fire. Dac's breathing labored with every step closer his brother took. "I knew I'd find you here," Luca said as he looked at his brother's weakened and frail figure sitting in a wooded rocking chair in the center of the room. "When was the last time you fed?"

"That's no concern of yours," Dac stopped rocking in his chair. "What are you doing here?" The last thing he was interested in was another encounter with his brother. "How did you find me?"

"Come on, brother. I'm worried about you. Come hunt with me." There was genuine concern in Luca's words. He stepped down from the last concrete step, though he stopped himself from getting any closer to his brother.

Dac was silent. The smell of human blood radiated from every pore in Luca's body. It was clear to Dac that Luca had already fed right before he showed up here at his place of dwelling. The hunger inside him stirred. He loathed and ached for it at the same time.

Dac stood up now. He stared back at his brother. His eye narrowed. Swiftly, he lunged at Luca, grabbing him by the hair and arching his head back. To his disappointment, Luca didn't struggle, nor did he resist as Dac sunk his teeth into the vein in his brother's neck. Deep down, Dac wanted to, no, he needed to, feel the power struggle between the two. He needed to feel his superiority over Luca. Luca had abandoned him long ago and then returned only to forcibly drag him into this existence of the vampire. He hated Luca for it. He always would. There was no way they could ever be brothers. Not the way Luca wanted.

With his brother's blood spilling down his throat, Dac felt his strength and power returning after weeks of not feeding. Sensations of thirst and hunger that he hadn't felt since his first days as a vampire awoke within him. He gripped tighter to the strands of hair entangled in his fingers before he tossed his brother across the room like a rag doll. Luca hit the ground with a thump.

"Feel better now?" Luca asked. His laugh was devilish, and his eyes glowed with red as he wiped the remnants of blood from his neck.

With his back turned to him, Dac twisted his head, taking one last glance at Luca, who was still seated on the cement floor. The taste of his blood still lingered in his mouth. He sneered at his brother and brushed his tongue across his top teeth. Then Dac disappeared up the stairs and into the darkness of night, leaving his brother alone on the damp cellar floor.

The dirt lifted up from the dry earth as he sped across the unfamiliar woods of the town he now inhabited. He weaved through the thick, sturdy trees. Stray branches cracked under his feet. Woodland creatures scurried away into their hiding places as he passed. Laughter echoed from somewhere in the distance. Dac couldn't tell how far off noise was, but he was sure he recognized the voice. He remembered the pink boots she wore on her tiny feet, her curly hair falling around her small face, and the sparkle of her bright blue eyes as she had stared up at him and Nikolai that night in front of her house. Her mother had called her Sophia.

The laughter was growing louder. Where was she? What was she doing out in the woods this time of night? *Please don't come closer.* Dac thought to himself. He stood still with his back against a tree. The light of the moon broke through the canopy of leaves above. A warm breeze came through, carrying with it more sounds of laughter. Dac kept his feet planted firmly on the ground. He dared not move as the sound of the little girl's laughter surrounded him from all directions. He covered his ears with his hands. *Sophia go home.* He silently pleaded.

The craving for human blood tormented him as he was reminded of his first kill. It was a young boy he encountered at the edge of the woods when he ran away from his brother's home deep in the mountains of their home country. The guilt and the pleasure of that moment remained a constant reminder of the monster his brother had made him. Every kill after was equally as harrowing until he had finally found a way to receive human blood without taking human life.

But tonight, the hunger growing inside him craved more than what a donation could supply. The blood he drank from his brother ignited a thirst for more than blood. He yearned for the very core of the human existence. It was the soul and spirit they consumed along with the blood when drinking from a mortal being that he was aching for now.

Shadows formed around him. The laughter disappeared. The moonlight faded. He was now standing in the total darkness and silence. He looked around but, even with his vampire sight, saw nothing. The air was too still. Someone supernatural was nearby. He could feel their preternatural presence, but who was it? Why couldn't he see them? Where was the little girl, Sophia? He couldn't let them get to her.

Suddenly the leaves of the trees rustled in the new incoming breeze. The shadows retreated. The light of the moon lit up the night sky once again. Whoever had been there was now gone. A melody traveled along the steady winds. It was a familiar sound though he could not place where he had heard it before, nor could he ignore it. Following the sound, Dac continued on through the woods. This time he strolled along, taking in the many scents and sounds of an outdoor nature he had long ago forgotten.

He walked for miles until he came upon a large stone wall. Behind that wall stood a familiar house. He climbed over the wall. Blue and clear lights lit up the windows of the large house. He listened for sounds inside. The song of a music box rang in his ears. He followed the melody to a widow at the back of the house. This was Sophia's room. The young girl sat on the floor of her room, playing with her dolls. The ballerina danced in circles inside the music box on her desk.

The craving for blood and life consumed him from the inside out. Dac leaned his back against the side of the house. He breathed in the warm night air. Sophia was safe for tonight, but he needed to leave from here before she wasn't.

Four

In the days since Cloe's death, sleep had pretty much eluded Jace. When he closed his eyes, his mind just replayed the images of finding Chloe in the bathtub. Visions of her lifeless body, the bloody water streaming out of the tub onto the floor, invaded his consciousness. Even in the moments where he had succumbed to sleep, he never found peace. Nightmares of the vampire assaulted his dreams. The glistening fangs dripped with blood. Cold hands gripped his neck. Faint screams rang out in the background. There was a clue somewhere in those screams. Something to do with Cloe's death. If only he could stay asleep long enough to hear what it was.

The pounding on his front door awoke him from his restless sleep. He wiped the sleep from his eyes and threw a wrinkled t-shirt over his bare chest. When he answered the door, Sarah was standing on the other side. The rays of the sun reflected off her coppery red hair like the halo of an angel. She held a tray of coffees in one hand and a plastic bag with two plastic containers in the other.

"Good morning, sunshine," she said as he stepped out of her way and let her in the house. He smirked and took the tray of coffee. He led her into the kitchen, where she put the bag on the table. "I brought breakfast," she continued when he hadn't said anything.

The scent of coffee and bacon filled the room as Sarah unpacked the containers. "Sorry, but what are you doing here?" Jace asked her.

"I told you breakfast." She replied. "Then we have somewhere to be. So, sit, eat, then get dressed."

"Where are we going?"

"To see my great grandmother. If you want to go after these vampires, then you need to be armed with more information than I can give you."

"If you say so, you're the expert."

"I'm no expert. If that were true, we wouldn't need my grandmother." Sarah winked.

"Still, thank you for everything." Jace took a sip from his coffee cup and picked at the food in front of him.

"Just eat and get dressed," Sarah smirked.

The drive to Sarah's great-grandmother's place felt endless. Trees lined the long stretch of highway. Grey storm clouds threatened the earlier blue summer sky. Jace peered out of the window of Sarah's car, thinking about his recent dreams. Across the medium, on the other side of the highway, a vehicle was stopped in the grass. Smoke rose out from under its smashed-up hood. The car's occupants stood anxiously waiting for their rescue. Traffic slowed as they passed by the accident, but it picked up again shortly after. They continued the rest of the way seamlessly.

Sarah's great-grandmother lived just outside of Aura City. When they pulled up to her house, Jace noticed the pink two-story cottage was in desperate need of repair. A single tree with blooming purple flowers stood amongst the brown dead grass and half bare shrubs that lined the stoned walkway. A small iron gate covered in ivy blocked the way to the front door.

Sarah reached over the gate, unlocking it from the other side so they could walk through. "I haven't been here in years," she whispered.

"Does she even know we're coming?" Jace asked.

"Not exactly," Sarah answered meekly.

"You don't think we should have called first?"

"Well, I wasn't sure she would agree to meet with us."

"What do you mean? Why wouldn't she meet with us?"

"Well, um, you see – well, she um...."

"She what, Sarah?"

"She's a bit reluctant to talk about vampires. She, matter of factly, told me to never ask her about them again. But that was a long time ago, and I was like ten, so...."

"Sarah," Jace sighed. He shook his head with frustration.

Sarah shrugged her shoulders and knocked on the door to the cottage. A woman in pink scrubs and a white knit cardigan answered the door.

"Can I help you?" The woman asked.

"Hi, may we speak with Brigid Higgins? I'm her granddaughter," Sarah replied.

"Granddaughter?" The woman cocked her head to the side as though she had no idea Brigid had a granddaughter.

"Yes. My name is Sarah. This is my friend Jace. May we see her please?" Sarah was persistent.

"Wait here, please. Let me see if she's available."

Jace stood next to Sarah on the woman's front porch. He picked at the dirt under his fingernails. The caretaker's tone made him even more nervous than he already was. He was prepared to turn around and leave when the door opened up again. An older woman stood before them. She wore her silver hair in a tight bun at the nape of her neck. She kept her glare down towards the floor. Her expression was not very welcoming. The wooden cane she leaned on threatened to break under her weight. She wasn't a very large woman but not petite either and appeared relatively strong for someone in her late nineties.

"Come on in," she said as she led them into the house. She walked with a slight limp to her left leg hence the cane, Jace thought.

In the front hallway stood an empty coat rack. An autumn fern was set on a table in the corner. A pendulum clock hung on the wall. The only light was that which came through the windows on either side of the front door.

Brigid led both Jace and Sarah into the living room. She sat down on the settee, resting her cane against the sidearm. Jace sat in the large armchair opposite her, and Sarah took the other chair next to Jace. Jace took note of the two side tables cluttered with unopened mail.

"So, Sarah, as lovely as it is to see you after all these years, I sense this isn't a social call, so what brings you here?" Brigid asked. She was clearly not the type to mince words, Jace thought to himself.

"You're right, grandmother. You see my friend Jace here; well, he needs your help?"

"Sarah, I'm just an old woman. I don't see much that I can do. What is it you think I can help with?"

"He just needs information, and you can provide him more than I can. Please, I wouldn't ask if it weren't important."

"What sort of information?"

"Everything you know about vampires."

"Sarah, we've spoken about this. I don't know anything. I can't help you." Brigid felt around with her hand for her cane. Her stare stayed fixed on where Sarah and Jace were seated across from her. This was when Jace realized the older woman needed the cane for more than just walking; she was blind.

"But grandmother, please, it's...."

"Leave it alone, Sarah." She stood up to leave, holding on to her cane. As she began to walk away, Jace stood up from his chair.

"Mrs. Higgins, please. I really need your help. My fiancée was killed by a vampire." Jace pleaded with her.

Brigid Higgins stopped. A flutter arose in his stomach as Jace thought for a moment that she had changed her mind and decided to help them, but then she continued out of the room. His shoulders slumped. This was a waste of time. They could be doing research at Sarah's shop with all the books on vampires and the occult that she kept there. There had to be something there that could help them.

Jace looked over at Sarah. She was already standing. She placed a hand on Jace's arm and said, "wait here." Then Sarah walked out of the room to search for her grandmother, leaving Jace alone in the living room.

Jace paced around the living room while he waited for Sarah to return, hopefully with Brigid. He stopped in front of the fireplace mantle, looking at the vintage art deco-style wooded radio placed on top of it. Jace wondered if it still worked. He went back to pacing, looking at the black and white family photos hanging on the walls. A dress form half draped in fabric was standing in the corner. A tape measure hung around its neck. Instinctively he reached out and felt the material. It felt soft like silk, but its weight felt heavier. He dropped the fabric fixing it back around the dress form, not wanting it to fall to the ground.

Jace walked over to the window and pulled open the curtain a bit so he could see out the glass. Outside dark grey shelf clouds were threatening the sky. A summer storm was inevitably on its way. Waiting was getting harder and harder the longer Sarah and her grandmother were gone. Jace didn't believe Sarah would be able to convince her grandmother to share whatever information she had about the vampires. She very clearly didn't want to talk about it, and given Sarah's earlier admission, she wasn't likely to change her mind.

Jace thought about when Sarah had asked him to sneak into the vampire house and get a look at their journals. He was reluctant to do it at the time, but he wondered now if that were possible. He thought about Emmaline and how she had been almost like a friend to him during his time there. Maybe he could use her to get access. Plus, Harper was back. Could he use his past friendship with her? Did she know about Cloe's death? Cloe had been her best friend once. Surely, she would help.

As Jace stood there reflecting about the past, contemplating what he could do if Brigid still refused to talk to them, he heard footsteps just outside the room. He turned around to see Sarah by the entryway. The woman standing next to her was not her grandmother, however. It was the nurse.

"She won't come back," Sarah said.

"It's best you two leave this alone. Nothing good can come of you asking these sorts of questions. Please just leave." The nurse said.

Jace nodded and followed Sarah out of the house. The nurse slammed the door behind them. The wind had really picked up since before they arrived, and the rain was beginning to fall. Jace expected the ride back home to feel much longer than the ride here, but then he noticed Sarah was driving in the wrong direction.

"Where are we going?" He asked her.

"There's a motel not far from here. I'm not giving up just yet. We'll try again tomorrow."

Jace shook his head. "Do you really think that's a good idea? She'll probably just shut the door in our face. If she even answers at all. Maybe we should go home."

"The storm's coming. Let's just wait until the morning, and we'll try one more time with my grandmother. If she still refuses to talk to us, we'll go home and come up with another plan."

"Fine." Jace agreed.

Once at the motel, Sarah got out of the car and walked over to the lobby. Jace had offered to go, but she insisted he stay in the car. He tried to give her money at least, but again she refused it. She came back and handed him a key card.

"I got us adjoining rooms." She told him.

By this time, the storm was really picking up. Fragile branches were being ripped from their trees. The rain was pouring down from the sky. Jace and Sarah ran through the puddles that covered the parking lot to the shelter of the motel to find their rooms.

Jace tore off his soaked shirt and threw it over the chair. He could hear Sarah in the next room using the cheap motel hairdryer. He settled onto the bed and turned on the tv. The wind and thunder were howling outside, and the lightning was lighting up the sky in electric colors of blue and white. Just then, the lights went out.

Sarah knocked on the adjoining door. When Jace opened it, she was standing there in just her T-shirt. Jace swallowed hard and shifted his glance away from her.

"Just got a voicemail from my grandmother. She said to come by tomorrow afternoon."

Five

They arrived at Sarah's grandmother's house the following afternoon. The nurse answered the door and led them directly to the living room, where Brigid was already waiting for them. Sarah greeted her grandmother as they entered the room. Brigid waved her off but motioned for them to sit. They each took the same seats as the day before.

"I thought it over last night and decided to share with you all that I know. But after today, don't come asking again. I will not speak on this again after today," Brigid began. "First, I will give you all the knowledge I have on the vampires and their existence, and then I will tell you how to hunt and destroy them. But believe me when I say it won't be easy. It takes a special kind of person to do what needs to be done, and the risk is great." Brigid paused to drink from the ceramic teacup that sat on the table next to her. The unopened letters that littered the table threatened to slide off the edge. Jace fought the urge to reach over and grab them. Instead, he chose to focus on Brigid as she continued talking.

"I understand you have already encountered a vampire, and that is what brings you here now," Brigid said. "I caution you to be careful as they most likely can see and hear everything you do and say. For that reason, I have taken measures within this room to block them out, and I will give you the tools to do the same for yourselves and your own living spaces.

Now understand there have been stories and folklore circulating since ancient times. Since the beginning, demons, evil non-human beings, and revenants have existed. They go by different names, and each requires different measures to ensure their survival. These creatures we call vampires come in two breeds, those who were born human and become vampires later and those that were never human at all. A vampire that was never human will be harder to destroy, but we will get to that later.

Most humans that become vampires do so because there is an exchange of blood with the vampire that creates them. The reason in which a vampire creates another depends on the individual vampire. Some do it for companionship or to strengthen their coven. Some bring over their family members or lovers unwilling to live through the centuries without them. But then there are those who are created from a curse. The curse of the seventh son." Brigid paused again, taking another sip from her cup, then placing it back on the table. This time a few of the envelopes did fall. They landed silently on the berber carpet covered floor. Brigid continued, ignoring the fallen pieces of mail. "If what Sarah told me yesterday is true, then you have already met one of them, so it is important for you to know their history. This is what I know of the story." A crash was heard from another room. Brigid, Sarah, and Jace each turned in the direction of the noise. The nurse called out her apologies, and they could hear her sweeping the broken glass into the trash bin. Brigid went back to telling her story while Jace and Sarah listened intently.

"They were a prominent family somewhere in the area that we know as modern-day Romania. Sometime in the late 15th Century, the head of the family, looking to keep the family's status during turbulent times, sought out the help of a demon. No one knows for sure the deal that was made, but the story says the demon turned him into an immortal, a vampire. However, he never made good on his end of the bargain, and instead, he killed the demon. But before the demon died, a spell was cast on the man. The spell said the man's seventh son would become a vampire at the age of twenty-six. The man would die, and the son would take over. This curse would repeat with every seventh son. Obsessed with his own immortality, the vampire killed his son the night before his twenty-sixth birthday. And every seventh son thereafter. After a while, members of the family were careful not to have too many children, that is until one was born 150 years later. His parents hid him and his oldest brother away with another family in one of the local villages. Some years later, the older brother discovered the secret and set out to claim his and his brother's place amongst the family. He destroyed the vampire and then drank his blood, becoming a vampire himself, eventually going back for his brother. He, too, however, became obsessed with the power of the vampire and murdered members of the family he felt were disloyal to him. Those he felt were loyal, he turned into vampires creating his own coven of vampires. The thing you need to understand most of all is that because of the demon's magic, these vampires are very powerful, as is any other vampire they make. And worse, they are almost indestructible."

"Almost? So, they can be destroyed?" Jace asked.

"Of course. Even the immortal aren't truly immortal."

So how can we kill them?"

"Be patient. I will get to that part. First, you need to understand their powers and what drives them."

"I'm sorry. Please continue." Jace apologized for interrupting, feeling slightly ashamed for his impatience.

"You should know that there are only a few of these vampires," Brigid went on, ignoring Jace's apology. "They are usually particular in who they create. And only those created by the two brothers can match their powers, strength, and immortality. But you should be aware that any vampire, no matter who their maker, will still be much stronger than yourself and hold certain abilities you as a human do not. When encountering any type of vampire, you must always exercise extreme caution."

"What about these other vampires, the ones that weren't born human?" Jace interrupted.

"We are not sure how these beings came into existence, but they are mere spiritual entities."

"Like ghosts?" Sarah asked.

"Similar in concept, I assume. But these creatures feed off the energies of living beings and can take on many different forms, human or animal. They do not need to drink blood from humans, but they can, and some do. The blood gives them a more human appearance but also strengthens them. Without human blood, they can survive, but they will be weaker. But don't be fooled; however, this doesn't make them easier to kill. Without blood, they remain invisible. Think of these beings as a deadly virus, an unseen killer."

"Can other vampires make themselves invisible?" Jace asked, thinking about that moment in the funeral home where he thought he felt a vampire touch him but didn't see them.

"In a way, yes, but it's more a trick of the mind than actual invisibility. They can affect how you perceive things and, in some cases, cause you to go into a trance-like state. They typically will use these tricks as a way to escape or to trap a victim. These are just some of the things they can do. They can move fast, covering great distances in a short amount of time. Some can read minds. As you know, if they bite you, they communicate with you but can also control you if they please to do so. There is a way to block this, however. You can use the things in this bag, and there are instructions written out in there as well." Brigid held out a small burlap bag. Jace gently grabbed it from her. He peeked inside the bag for a moment and then placed it on the floor next to his feet.

"Now, where was I?" Brigid continued. "Oh, that's right, the powers of the vampire. Some vampires can control animals, and some can control the weather, but these last two are rare. And if you were to strip them of all these things, they are not much different than you or

I. They are driven by emotion, power, and the will to survive. They cry. They feel pain. They bleed. But they also heal fast, although they are not completely invulnerable."

"Like the oils," Jace commented.

"Exactly. The oils, garlic, and hawthorn cause an allergic-like reaction. When they come in contact with the skin, it will burn and blister. If they come in contact with the bloodstream or are somehow ingested, they cause a reaction similar to anaphylactic shock. All of these things the vampires can heal from, but how long that healing takes depends on the amount of contact. This is why these are only used as repellents or a way to slow them down."

"What about the stake to the heart and the sun?" Jace asked.

"The heart, like any other organ within the vampire, will heal itself eventually. Piercing the heart will not likely kill a vampire but will render him immobile for a time."

"How long?" Sarah asked.

"Could be weeks, months, or even years."

"And the sun?" Jace asked again.

"The sun weakens them. The higher in the sky the sun is, the weaker the vampire is. During this time, they sleep and recharge."

"So, it doesn't kill them?"

"Not instantly. Their skin is sensitive to the sun, and it will cause a server burn injury to the vampire, but they can most times heal from it. There are only a few records of a vampire dying by sunlight. These vampires were captured and imprisoned outside without shelter from the sun. They suffered days like this until they finally perished."

Jace cringed at the thought of it. He pictured Harper or Emmaline lying in a field somewhere, totally exposed to the elements of the harsh sunlight, the rays scorching their skin. Then he asked, "how do you kill them then?"

"The only true way to kill the vampire is to sever the head from the spine."

Both Jace and Sarah shuddered.

"Hunting and killing the vampire isn't for the faint of heart," Brigid said. "If you are going to embark on this journey, you must have a strong will and a strong stomach." That was the last she said. She reached for her walking stick, stood up from her chair, and left the room.

Jace and Sarah looked at each other. Neither of them knowing exactly what the other was thinking. They sat in silence for a minute. Jace finally stood up. He looked around the room one more time.

"I guess we should go," he said.

"Yea, I suppose you're right," Sarah replied as she, too, stood up from where she had been seated.

Jace snatched up the burlap bag Brigid had handed him only moments ago and followed Sarah out of the door.

BACK AT HOME, JACE stared at the contents spread out across his kitchen table. There was the cross necklace and oils Sarah had first given him, the hawthorn branches he'd picked up before going to Cloe's that fateful day she had killed herself in the bathtub, and the objects gifted to him earlier by Sarah's great grandmother Brigid. The bag Brigid handed him contained a silver amulet with three stones, a tiger eye, aquamarine, and obsidian. There was also a jar of cream made from white sage, hyssop, and eucalyptus and a spray containing the same ingredients. The instructions in the bag said for him to wear the necklace at all times and rub the cream into the scars on his neck and at each of his pulse points. It said to use the spray daily in every room of his house. Each of these things would offer himself and his home protection and free him from the hold of the vampire.

He wondered how Brigid knew about the scars on his neck. Sarah must have told her he had been bitten. He also wondered if this cream would stop the dreams he had been having. There was something in those dreams he was supposed to know. He felt it in his bones.

Somewhere in there was the clue to finding Cloe's killer. Should he risk it, losing the dreams, to protect himself? No, was the only answer he could come to. There had to be another way to close off his thoughts and hide his true intentions. For now, he put the amulet and cream back in the burlap bag and stored it on the shelf. He placed the hawthorn on each of the windows around his home. He put the old vials of oils in his pockets, hung the crucifix necklace around his neck, and walked out the door.

The night was clear, and the perfect temperature for riding with the windows rolled down. The breeze flowing into the car helped to clear his thoughts. The highway into Aura City was unusually deserted. He seemed to be the only one on the road besides the occasional car passing in the opposite direction. It felt peaceful, like the calm before the storm. A storm he knew was coming after tonight. But also, it felt like the first moment of peace he'd felt in weeks. It was as if the cloud hovering over him was beginning to clear, and the path before him was now visible.

Six

She stared down at the black stains on the floor, then at the dagger in her hand. The leather-wrapped handle felt warm against her cold skin. Every night for weeks, she held onto this same dagger as she swiped its hard steel blade across her flesh. The wound on her hand from the other night was beginning to heal. This time she lifted the t-shirt she wore and swiped the blade across the flesh covering her ribcage. The blood ran cold as it trickled down her skin. She made another cut just below the first and then two more. She watched as the blood ran down like rain against a window. The deep red color turned to black like tar as the air hit it, and it stained her skin.

She dipped her finger in the blood on her skin, then swiped her fingertips across the white canvas that leaned against her bedroom wall. Swirls of black and red created abstract designs. What she used to paint in acrylics and gouache, she now painted in blood. A fitting aesthetic, she thought.

The superficial wounds she created in her body healed just as quickly as she made them, but the bloodstains remained as a reminder of what she was, a monster. A monster who hurt those she cared about. She had been warned against her past actions, but she hadn't listened. Why had she come back here? She should have gone somewhere far away. But she was a coward. Yes, that's what she was a monster and a coward. Again, she swiped the blade across her stomach with one swift motion. A banging sound pounded against her brain as the blood rained down. Her vision blurred. The pounding grew louder and louder. A soft, lyrical sound vibrated along with the pounding in her

35

head. The door. The pounding was coming from the door. Someone was there, knocking and calling her name.

Harper tugged on her shirt, covering the fresh cuts she had just made across her stomach. She pulled the black sheet over the bloodstained canvas, then answered the door as she regained her composure. Emmaline was standing on the other side. She was dressed in one of her usual knee-length lace dresses and adorned in jewelry. Instead of her long red hair falling down past her shoulders, tonight, she wore it wrapped up on top of her head. Harper gave what she hoped was an inviting smile.

"Quentin asked me to invite you to the dining room. He thought it would be nice if the three of us drank together tonight. Maybe it could bring us a little bit of normalcy." Emmaline said.

"Yea, sure, normalcy." Harper rolled her eyes.

"Are you ok?" Emmaline asked her.

"Yea, fine," Harper answered unconvincingly.

"Please come sit with us. It'll make you feel better." Emmaline pleaded with her.

"I'll be up in a few minutes." Shutting the door in Emmaline's face, Harper looked down at her blood-stained skin underneath her t-shirt before wiping it clean.

She changed her clothes into something more presentable, a pair of black jeans and a black v-neck blouse. Around her throat, she attached her black velvet choker. The same choker she had worn almost daily since becoming a vampire. She had bought it during her very first outing with Emmaline and Nikolai as a symbol of the captivity she felt. She smoothed her hair down and slipped on a pair of plain black ballet flats just like Cloe, her old best friend, used to wear.

Upstairs in the dining room, Quentin and Emmaline were already waiting in their usual seats. The chandelier that hung from the ceiling lit up the room. Flames flickered from the candles on the table. Quentin had set up everything just as they always had. The only thing

36

missing was their two friends, Dac and Nikolai. It was strange being in this room without them. It was strange being in this house without them. They owned this house and brought the rest of them here, giving them each a safe place from the outside world. Even though Nikolai technically was in the house, he had been unconscious since they returned from Noxwood, making it feel as though he wasn't there.

Harper brushed her hand across the back of the chairs as she walked past Nikolai's and Dac's empty seats. An ache settled in her heart. She felt like she'd been gut-punched as the guilt established itself in the pit of her stomach. The smell of blood rose from the glasses on the table to her nose. She took her place at the table. The hunger inside her was unmistakable. So much stronger than she had realized. She picked up the glass in front of her and took a sip. The deep red liquid was thick, sweet, and warm. But it was missing something. It was missing the essence of human life. She sighed as she placed the glass back on the table.

"How is Nikolai today?" She asked.

"The same, unfortunately, but I can feel him healing," Quentin tried to be reassuring.

"It's nice to have the three of us together. And of course, it will be even better once Nikolai is better and Dac comes back," Emmaline said. "Do you think Dac will come home soon?" She asked.

"I'm not sure when he'll be back. He has a lot to work out with his brother," Quentin said.

"Yea, but it's been weeks already, and I thought he'd be back by now. He hasn't even checked on Nikolai. It just doesn't make sense to me that he'd stay away from us this long. He is coming back, isn't he?"

"I don't know." Quentin's voice was sympathetic as he answered Emmaline's questions, but Harper could tell he was growing impatient.

"What happened out there in Noxwood? What aren't you telling me?" Clearly, Emmaline had sensed Quentin's impatience too. She slammed her hand down on the table, demanding an answer. The glasses rattled. The flames of the candlesticks flickered as they threatened to tip over.

"Leave it alone, Emmaline. Our concern right now needs to be about healing Nikolai," Quentin scolded her, his impatience finally reaching its breaking point. He stood up and stormed out of the room.

"So much for dinner like the old days," Harper raised an eyebrow, looking at Emmaline as she raised her glass to her lips, taking yet another sip of the lifeless blood inside it.

"I'm sorry. But I know you guys are keeping something from me. I know Nikolai's wife and son are alive, and she stabbed him. I know they were behind all that happened before, and Luca only helped them. But that's all you guys have told me, and I know there's more to the story. What is really keeping Dac away? Why won't he come home?" Emmaline expected answers from Harper, but she wasn't yet ready to give them to her.

"You don't need to be sorry, but Quentin is right. You need to leave this alone." Harper told her.

Emmaline exhaled a harsh breath expressing her disappointment.

"I should go too. I need some fresh air," Harper said as she got up from the table.

"Can I come with you?" Emmaline stood and followed her.

Harper didn't really want her tagging along, but she said, "Sure."

As they stepped outside into the warm summer night, a dark-colored car crept passed the house. That shouldn't have seemed unusual, but the slow speed at which the vehicle passed gave them pause. They stood at the doorstep for a moment before continuing on. When it seemed the car was gone, they walked down the path to the sidewalk. They decided to follow the direction the car had driven. By the time they had reached the corner, however, the car was nowhere in sight.

"Did that car seem strange to you?" Emmaline asked Harper.

"Yes, but more so that I couldn't get any kind of read on it," Harper replied.

"Same here."

"But it did seem vaguely familiar like I've seen it before." Harper racked her brain, trying to remember where she may have seen that car, but she just couldn't place it.

"Interesting. You think it's someone you know?"

"I'm not sure, but maybe we should keep watch for it. See if it comes past the house again."

"Yeah, maybe. Should we tell Quentin?"

"If we see it again. Let's not worry him if we don't have to. He has enough on his plate looking after Nikolai." Something about the car bugged her, but Harper didn't want to bother Quentin with it if it turned out to be nothing.

"Yeah, true." Emmaline agreed.

They walked the next few blocks in silence. For a brief moment, the strange car had distracted Harper from the real reason she had wanted to go out, but with each passing human on the street, the feelings of thirst crept back in. The problem was Emmaline was with her, so she had to suppress the desire she felt to feed on human life until another time. Unless she could somehow lead her away for a few minutes, she didn't need very long, just long enough to grab some unsuspecting human and drink its blood. Then she got an idea.

"Hey, do you feel that?" Harper asked Emmaline.

"Feel what?"

"I don't know exactly. I just got this feeling like someone's watching us." Harper tried to make her voice sound troubled.

"Probably because of the car earlier."

"Yeah, you're probably right. But maybe we should check just in case." Harper urged her.

"I'm sure it's fine." Emmaline tried reassuring her. To Harper's annoyance, Emmaline didn't seem to be taking the bait, but she pressed on.

"Just to be sure, do you mind checking down that street?" Harper was growing frustrated with Emmaline's constant reassurances. She just needed to get her out of the way for a few minutes. "I'll check down this way," she said as she pointed in the opposite direction she was sending Emmaline.

"Yeah, sure. I'll take a look, but like I said, I'm sure everything's fine."

"Thanks." Harper gave her a smile, and Emmaline turned down the street in search of some imaginary person.

With Emmaline now out of the way, Harper took off down the darkened street. She ordinarily would not hunt this close to home, but tonight she had no choice. She ducked down into the dark underground stairwell of a closed storefront. Behind the green painted steel door lay a storage room. Shelves lined the concrete walls. They were stacked with canned goods and paper products. Roaches scattered about, scavenging for their next meal. Large black garbage bags had been tossed carelessly on the floor. She tried to block out the stench of rotting old fruits, vegetables, and other spoiled foods.

The sound of human footsteps radiated through the street above her. She didn't have much time before Emmaline would come looking for her. She had to make her move quickly. She lingered at the opening of the stairwell. She watched as people passed by until she finally saw her mark. A single pair of footsteps crossed her path. She snatched the person by the ankle and dragged her down into the underground storage room. Her head hit the pavement on the way down. The young woman's blonde hair was tied up in a bun on top of her head, neatly exposing the vein in her neck. Harper allowed no time for the girl to put up a fight. She swiftly sank her teeth into her neck, immersing herself in the experience.

A shadow passed in the night above her. Hurriedly she dropped the body she held in her arms. It fell to the ground with a thump. The deep blue eyes were wide open, staring back at Harper. She bent down, gently closing the eyelids. She wiped the blood from her mouth using the fabric from the girl's shirt, then ascended back up to the street. Emmaline was there waiting for her.

"What were you doing down there?" Emmaline asked when she saw Harper approach from the stairwell.

"I thought I saw someone go down there, but there was nothing. I guess you were right. It's just my nerves playing tricks on me." Harper gave her a reassuring nudge.

"It's understandable. You've been through a lot lately. Maybe we should go back to the house." Emmaline innocently suggested.

"Yea, I think you're right. Let's get home."

As they walked back towards the house, Harper glanced back at the dark stairway, where behind the cold steel door lay the dead body of a young woman. She would have to come back later and take care of that.

JACE SAW HARPER AND Emmaline leave the vampire house. He only hoped they did not notice him yet. He circled the block with his car one more time before deciding to sit and wait. He parked his car a couple of feet away from where he could watch for the two ladies to come home, not yet sure how he wanted to approach them. What he did know was that he had to be careful not to sneak up on them. He remembered what happened last time when he surprised Nikolai and Dac out in Noxwood. Nikolai almost strangled him to death.

He sat patiently in the car, watching the street in the dark, trying his best to keep his mind clear. He inhaled deep breaths in and exhaled each slowly out. With each breath, he relaxed his muscles clearing out the stress both physically and mentally. It was the only way he knew to block his thoughts from the vampire. He had read about this theory in the book Sarah had given him when he first met her at her shop, and since he wasn't ready to try the cream potion from Sarah's great grandmother, this was the only trick he currently had at his disposal. So, he let the night breeze brush against his face from the open car window. He rested his head against the seat and stared off into the distance removing all thoughts from his mind with each meditated moment.

The long shadows coming toward him awoke him from his meditative state. He could not see who the shadows belonged to though they grew lengthier as they came closer. All around him, he was surrounded by darkness. The air outside the car grew still. His heart rate began to pick up. He searched around him for the owners of the shadows twisting his head from side to side, but he saw no one. Then a burst of laughter startled him so that he twitched in his seat. To his left, a couple of teenagers passed by, laughing and joking. Jace breathed a sigh of relief.

Maybe this decision to wait for Harper and Emmaline wasn't such a great idea, after all, he thought to himself. He contemplated going back home. His hands placed on the car keys; he was just about to restart the car's engine when he saw them.

He pulled in a sharp breath and opened the car door. He stepped out into the dark night. Then called her name.

"Emmaline!" Jace shouted out to her. The vampire turned her gaze in his direction. Her bright eyes shined through the black night, and her glowing skin reflected the moonlight. Within a moment, she was at his side.

"Jace. What are you doing here?" She asked.

"Looking for you."

Seven

The sound of the music box played in his ear. Why was he still hearing that sound? And the laughter, where was the laughter coming from? He thought he'd be safe deep in his cellar, but he couldn't escape the noise. The noise was everywhere. It had leached onto his mind like a parasite. His hands shook at his sides. He paced the cellar floor back and forth, sweeping his feet across the harsh concrete. His rat companion stayed in its corner, following his movements with its tiny beady eyes.

Luca must be the cause of this. He must be putting these sounds in his head somehow. That couldn't be "the music box" in the little girl's room. He had to find Luca and put a stop to this. But he was weak. He needed to feed first. It had been weeks since he'd adequately fed. The stash of blood he brought with him when he first arrived in Noxwood was long gone. He refused to take the blood directly from a human, and the blood he had taken from Luca the night before was not enough to sustain him through the night.

Dac looked over at the rat in the corner, and it scurried away. He could have caught it if he had wanted to, but he let it go. He took the steps one at a time until he reached the main floor of the house he dwelled underneath. He shuffled outside and into the thick woods, stalking around for his prey. The fragrant earth filled his vampiric senses. A rustling nearby alerted him to just the thing he was looking for. Dirt and leaves covered its grey and black fur. Its tiny paws continued to dig into the soil, unaware of Dac's presence.

Dac reached down and grabbed the raccoon. Its startling squeal was quickly extinguished by Dac's bite. He ripped into the creature's flesh, its fresh blood spilling into his mouth. The taste was bitter yet vaguely satisfying. He could feel some of his strength returning. He dropped the animal to the ground. The music and laughter in his head had ceased for the moment. Now it was time to visit his brother.

As he reached the gated property of his brother's home, he was flooded with memories of not only months ago but centuries past when he lived in Romania. He'd always known a time may come when he would have to reckon with his past, although he never expected what happened last winter. Now it was time to settle things with his brother. Too bad his friendship with Nikolai was now lost forever. He was sure Nikolai would survive the attack, and it was only a matter of time before Quentin told him the whole truth if he hadn't already.

Unlike his brother, who had just entered his home uninvited a couple of nights earlier, Dac knocked on the door. He knew someone was there. He sensed the presence of other vampires. Finally, the door opened. On the other side stood a woman, pale-faced with long dark hair. She had features just like Harper. Or was it that Harper had features just like her? Either way, there she was, the woman who was supposed to be dead—the same woman who had stabbed his best friend.

"Una," he said. His voice full of the contempt he felt.

"I suppose you have come for Luca. Please come in." She was nauseatingly polite and gestured for him to enter the house. She led him into the front sitting room. Luca was standing next to the window peering behind the curtain. He turned to face them. Una retreated from the room, leaving Luca and Dac alone. The room smelled of burned candle wax and jasmine. Two oversized chairs sat in opposite corners, and a small sofa was set in the middle of the room. An upright piano was against the far wall.

"I see your pretentiousness hasn't faded," Dac said to his brother.

"Nice to see you too, brother. I knew it was only a matter of time before you showed up again. Have you come to join us?"

"Hardly."

"Then why are you here?" Luca asked disdainfully.

"I want answers, Luca. What have you done to me?"

"What are you talking about? I haven't done anything to you."

"Then why am I hearing these voices and this music in my head? I know it is you. It only started after you came by last night."

"If you are going mad, that has nothing to do with me," Luca said as he strolled over to the sofa and sat down, stretching his legs across the full length of the settee. "Now, if you haven't come to make nice, then please see yourself out."

Dac lunged at Luca in frustration, grabbing him by his shirt collar and lifting him up from his seat. At that exact moment, Lizbeth and Sonya entered the room. The glow in Luca's eyes turned to red. Dac released his grip on Luca's shirt, dropping him back on the sofa. Luca lept up enraged.

"You have always blamed me for your problems. You've made me out to be the bad guy when all I've ever done was to protect you," Luca shouted.

"Protect me? Ha, that's a laugh. I am what I am because of you."

"You are what you are because of a curse, because of when you were born and who you were born to. You were always meant to be a vampire. You would have died if not for me."

"Maybe you should have let me die."

"Maybe I should have. Now leave." Luca stretched out his arm, pointing to the door.

Dac turned and stormed out of the house, slamming the door behind him. The night blurred as he raced through the darkness. A swarm of bats flew above him. Dogs howled in the background. The flush heat of fury ran through him in contrast to the cold, undead flesh that encased his bones. The feeling reminiscent of a feverish cold sweat.

Once he reached the woods, he dropped to the ground pounding his fists into the dirt.

The song of the music box started up in his head again as if being carried by the wind. The sounds of little Sophia's laughter carried along with it. "Shut up, shut up," he whispered to himself, his hands covering his ears. He shook his head from side to side. He felt the hard nudge of a boot against his hip, and when he looked up, Luca was standing over him.

"Get up," Luca said as he offered Dac his hand.

Dac grabbed his hand, accepting his brother's assistance. They walked through the wood in complete silence until they reached the house where Dac had been staying. The house remained mainly unfurnished except for the few pieces of furniture left behind by the previous owners. Luckily, those things included a sofa and chair. Dac sat on the couch while Luca took the chair. Neither man turned on the light. They remained seated in the dark, staring at each other, until finally, Dac chose to speak.

"Why did you follow me?"

"Because I know you, little brother, probably more than you know yourself, and I remember the night I came to you after both our parents had died. You were alone in that room, succumbing to your despair. Tonight, I saw that same look on your face that I saw back then."

"Why did you come to my room that night? After all those years of being gone, why then?"

"Are you finally ready to hear the story? Are you done pushing me away?"

"Yes. I'm ready." Dac sighed and dropped his head in defeat of his usual defiance.

"It's simple, really," Luca shifted in his chair. "The night before I left, someone had come to the house looking for you. I heard our father arguing with the man who stood outside our door. As I was trying to listen, our mother caught me eavesdropping. She sent me to my room, but I wouldn't let up. I had to know what this man wanted, why he had come searching for you. Finally, she told me about the curse. She explained to me how she and our father weren't our biological parents and told me we needed to protect you. Later that night, I left out the window to find this man, the vampire. I convinced him to turn me, that I would help him get to you. I patiently waited while my powers grew over the years. Then the time finally came. I destroyed him, and I came back for you. The rest you already know."

"So that's it? That's the story?" Dac asked.

"That's the story," Luca replied.

"But I don't get it. The curse has to do with a seventh son. There are only two of us."

"Hadn't you ever wondered about our age difference, why there are so many years between us? The others died soon after being born. You are the seventh son."

"I guess I never thought about it."

"Well, I haven't come here to reminisce about the past. I told you all you need to know about that. I came here to warn you that you are still in danger. Alex is still after you and Nikolai, and if he manages to get to your injured friend, he will finish the job Una couldn't."

"Can't you keep your minions under control?"

"No more than you can yours, brother." Luca stood from the chair he had been seated in and disappeared out the door.

Dac sat in the dark empty room, thinking about his brother's warning. If Alex was looking to destroy him, then he must be responsible for the music and laughter in his head. Now armed with this new information, it was time to go home and face whatever was waiting for him there.

"JACE, I DON'T KNOW if I can help you. I mean, what you're asking is crazy." Emmaline said.

"I know, and I wouldn't be asking if it weren't important. Besides, you said it yourself, Dac and Nikolai were vampires who hunted other vampires. I'm only asking for the same favor. I helped them when they were looking for Dac's brother last winter. I only need to know who killed Cloe."

"Yes, but you are a human; it's different. Besides, Dac hasn't come home from Noxwood, and Nikolai hasn't yet recovered."

"What are you talking about? What happened to Nikolai?" Emmaline's last message to Jace had said things weren't that great when everyone had gotten back from Noxwood, but she hadn't said anyone was hurt. As Emmaline filled him in, his heart ached a little for Nikolai. He was filled with a mix of surprise and confusion. "So, his wife and son are alive? That must have been a shock."

"Must have been more shocking to find out they wanted to kill him. But there's more that happened out there that Quentin and Harper won't tell me. And Harper is different ever since she came back. I think it's best if you go home, Jace and please just leave all this behind you. I'm really sorry for your loss, but you must move on with your life. Forget about us and forget about vampires. Keep yourself safe. I'm sure it's what your fiancée would have wanted." Emmaline was as polite and friendly as always. There was a genuine sense of caring in her tone, but this wasn't the response he was hoping to get from her.

"Thanks. You're right. I shouldn't have come," Jace got back inside of his car. Emmaline looked empathic to his plight, but instead of changing her mind and offering to help, she swiftly made her way inside the vampire house. Harper was still standing out on the sidewalk in the exact spot she had stopped when Jace had called out to Emmaline. Jace found it somewhat strange that she hadn't come over, but he was sure she was listening, nonetheless.

On the drive back home, Jace replayed his conversation with Emmaline over in his head. It had been a mistake to go there. He knew it earlier, but he knew it even more now. He should have better prepared himself for what to say. All he really wanted was access to the house once again. Instead, he just blurted all the words out as if he were talking to an old friend. But Sarah and her grandmother were right. The vampires weren't his friends.

When Jace returned home, he flicked the switch on his living room wall to turn on the light, but the room remained dark. He reached for his phone to use its flashlight, but a voice spoke out, "Don't." The deep penetrating voice was unfamiliar to him. But he knew it was the voice of a vampire.

Jace froze in the doorway. The vampire spoke again, "Close the door." Jace did as he was told, though he kept his hand on the doorknob. He did so as much in the event he needed to make a quick getaway as it was to steady himself. He wasn't exactly sure he'd be able to get away even if he wanted to. His mind was now racing trying to determine what the vampire wanted. Was he here to kill him? Had he somehow overheard his conversation with Emmaline? But how could he have, and who even was he?

"Who are you, and what are you doing here?" Jace asked, trying his best to keep his voice steady.

"I came to make a deal," the vampire answered.

"A deal with me?" Jace asked.

"Yes, a deal with you. I'll help you find your vampire if you help me get rid of mine. But you have to keep your little vampire hunter friend away."

"I'd ask how you know I'm searching for a vampire, but you've probably read my mind. That is what you do, isn't it?"

"Actually, I heard you talking to the girl outside my brother's house."

"You're brother's house?" Jace asked, surprised. "Then you must be Luca?"

"Good guess. Yes, I am."

"I thought your brother was still in Noxwood. What were you doing there? I won't help you kill any of them." The words fell out of his mouth in a rambling expression of worry and concern. There was no denying Jace had grown to care for the vampires he had helped this past winter.

Luca laughed. "None of them are in any danger from me. But my brother is still in danger from another, so I went there looking for help since he is refusing to help himself. That is when I saw you, and I followed you back here. So, do we have a deal, or am I going to have to kill you?"

"Kill me?" Jace's voice cracked. He swallowed whatever saliva had formed in his mouth. His hand still clutching the doorknob, he grasped it tighter.

"Well, I can't exactly have you just going around hunting and killing vampires now, can I? How am I to know you wouldn't come after the rest of us after you have found the one you're seeking?"

"Well, I guess I have no choice then, do I?" Jace cleared his drying throat. "Ok. We have a deal. What do you want me to do?" He tried to disguise the dread in his voice when he spoke, though he feared he was unsuccessful.

"We'll discuss the details tomorrow night. I'll be back then. In the meantime, you may want to better prep your house. I'll be sure to allow you to invite me in next time."

The lights flickered on. Luca was gone. Jace wasn't sure how he left or how he had gotten in the hose in the first place. This little interaction had him feeling a bit unsettled. He took Luca's advice and gathered all the oils and the rest of the Hawthorne he had acquired from Sarah and spread them around the remaining entry points of his house before going to bed.

Eight

Trying to make his life feel somewhat normal, Jace decided to go into work. He made his morning coffee and put it in a thermos. Once he got to the office, he opened the laptop that sat on his desk. Emails from prospective clients had sat unread in his inbox for days. He spent all morning responding to each and every one of them. He welcomed the distraction, but his mind was still on his surprise visit from Luca the night before. He made it about halfway through the day before Alan convinced him to go back home. He spent the remainder of the afternoon avoiding Sarah and waiting for that inevitable moment when Luca showed up at his doorstep.

As darkness fell, his nerves became unsteady. He spent hours alone, just himself and the thoughts inside of his head. What was Luca going to ask him to do? And could he trust him? Would Luca keep his end of the bargain and find Cloe's killer? Would he kill him once he'd done his part? The only thing Jace knew for sure was he didn't want Luca in his head. He paced around the house, checking that all the hawthorn branches were in their places at the windowsills. He found the cream from Sarah's grandmother and rubbed it across his neck, temples, and wrists. He added the essential oils to all the same areas and put the necklace Sarah gave to him last winter around his neck along with the one from her grandmother. He was as prepared as he was going to get. There was nothing more to do until Luca showed up.

A shadow passed by the window. Jace's heart skipped a beat. He froze for a moment anticipating the knock on the door. When none came, he rushed over to the window peeking out of the blinds. He could see nothing outside in the darkness. He slumped onto the couch and waited impatiently for Luca's arrival.

He tried distracting himself by watching tv and scrolling through his phone, but nothing seemed to calm his nerves or his mind. His legs shook faster with each passing moment. Outside he could hear the wind picking up, but there was no mention of a storm coming. He went to the door opening it slowly to have a look outside. Just as he stepped out the door, a dark figure appeared before him like magic. Jace had never even seen the man walk up towards him. He let out a short gasp.

"Relax. I told you last night I won't hurt you. At least not yet," Luca winked. "Let's go inside." He gestured towards the door. Jace stepped aside, allowing Luca to enter the house first. The lights were on tonight, unlike last when Luca made him keep them off. With the element of surprise gone, Jace tried to keep his cool which was always tricky in the presence of a vampire. Especially one rumored to be so savage.

Jace vaguely remembered Luca being at the poker game last winter. The one he had been forced to attend. The same one which Zaine had attended. The same game Harper had followed him home from, bringing him into this nightmare reality full of mythical creatures who turned out to be not so fictional after all.

It was dark in the warehouse that night, and Luca sat at a desk in the far corner. Jace had barely had a good look at him then, but tonight he could see Luca's close resemblance to Dac. They had the same dark hair and translucent greyish skin, which Jace came to realize was common among vampires when they hadn't yet fed. They shared similar facial features, but Luca's eyes appeared darker and more deadly, with a red glow inside his pupils. Dac was intimidating, but Luca was downright horrifying.

Luca made himself comfortable tonight, taking a seat on Jace's couch. Jace sat on the chair next to him. He faced the vampire, his hands folded in his lap and his fingers fidgety as he tried to control the shaking in his leg. Finally, the vampire spoke.

"I guess I should tell you that I knew who you were when I invited you to the poker game last winter." He started, sensing Jace's recognition of him. "I knew you had been friends with Harper, and that's the reason I invited you. I knew Harper had been following Zaine, and when she saw you there, she would follow you instead of him. And I knew that when I took her friend Quentin, she would go to you for help before going to her vampire friends. Everything was carefully planned out then, but that isn't the reason I'm here now. I know the girl told you the other night about Alex and what happened back in Noxwood. That is why I am here. Quentin was draining Alex's energy as they were fighting that night, but when Nikolai was stabbed, Alex took advantage of the distraction and managed to get away. The problem is no one knows where Alex is now. The only one who has been in contact with him is his mother, Una. However, she claims not to know where he's hiding out. Anyway, it has recently come to my attention that Alex is still a threat to my brother Dac and also to Nikolai. While I may not care what happens to Nikolai, I do care what happens to my brother. That is where you come in," Luca explained.

"I don't understand. What exactly do you think I can do? And if you know who the threat is, why don't you just take care of him yourself?" Jace started to relax a bit, realizing, at least for now, that Luca needed him. However, he wasn't quite sure why. "Aren't you this almighty powerful vampire?"

"Your sarcasm will get you nowhere, boy." Luca sneered. His brows drew close; the red glow flickered like lightning in his eyes, and Jace quavered. "The only thing you need to understand is that like humans, we vampires also have rules and codes that we live by. Had it not been for Alex, I'd still be buried deep in the ground."

Jace found himself trying to understand. Here was this vicious and powerful vampire sitting across from him inside his house, asking him for help. He who was merely a human and certainly not as strong as the creature sitting on his couch. "So basically, you're saying you owe Alex your life?"

"Precisely. But you do not." Luca raised an eyebrow when he spoke these words.

"How did you survive? I mean, how did Alex save you, and why not the others?" Jace asked with genuine curiosity.

"I really don't think that's important."

"Well, I think that it is. If I'm going to go after this vampire for you, then I think I should know as much about him as possible." Jace was standing his ground.

"Fine then, I'll tell you. Your friends Dac and Nikolai killed most of my vampire coven before they got to me. Lizbeth, Sonya, and Una were the only three that escaped. Now I don't know if Dac didn't understand at that time the proper and only way to actually kill a vampire. I assume he did since he managed to destroy the others. Maybe when he got to me, he just couldn't go through it. Or maybe his plan was to leave me to suffer. Either way, he and his friend Nikolai put me in that grave to live out my days once the stab wounds healed and the poisons wore off. I would have spent eternity in the ground, not dead but not alive, with no blood to sustain me. It had been years that I stayed trapped in there, just a mind inside an immobile, immortal body. Every breath bringing dirt into my lungs. The same dirt that was grating against my skin. In the beginning, I tried to claw my way out, but I was too weak.

Eventually, I fell into a deep sleep until one day I felt a cool breeze against my back. I was able to turn my body for the first time in ages. My eyes finally opened, and there was a young vampire standing over me, offering his hand to help me out of the grave. He brought me back to my house, where he, Lizbeth, Sonya, and Una all helped to nurse me back to health. It took years for me to fully recover my strength and even longer to get my full power restored. Once I did, that is when they all informed me of who Alex really was and of his plan. They needed me because none of them would be strong enough to go up against

Dac and because Nikolai was made from Dac's blood, he too would be a difficult opponent. Lizbeth and Sonya, like the others in my coven, had come to me looking for a place to belong. They felt safe with me knowing I had destroyed my ancestor. I then became their protector. Lizbeth made Una, and Una turned Alex. But I myself have made very few vampires during my long existence. Two, to be exact, Dac and the young girl Emmaline. So, you see, none of them were made from me, despite what legends you may have heard, so they do not have the demon blood nor the demon's power running through them. But that is a story for another time. Anyway, I went along with their plan always with the intention to reunite with my brother. To save his immortal soul. I may be the one with the demon inside of me, but Dac is the one who is truly evil." Luca leaned forward, resting his elbows on bent knees.

"The demon?" Jace's eyes grew wide.

"Yes, the demon. I thought your vampire hunting friend would have told you about that."

"She mentioned it, but I'd rather hear your side of the story. You know legends and all are usually missing actual facts." The curiosity was taking over and becoming more than a simple quest for information. Jace was now fueled by a bona fide interest in Luca's history. He wondered now if there were more to Luca than the evil legends described.

"Fine, then let me fill you in," Luca straightened out his posture again. "When my ancestor killed the demon, he removed and devoured the demon's heart. That is where the source of all his great power came from, so when I killed him, I did the same."

"And that is where your power comes from, makes sense."

"Exactly, but with Dac, he is the recipient of the curse. I believe he felt that if he killed me, he could kill the curse."

"But you're saying it won't?"

"No, it will not. The evil inside him is inherent. It was always there, but he always fights until it serves his purpose. The only way to kill the curse is to kill Dac, which is exactly what my ancestor would have done had I not killed him first. I thought that if I were to become a vampire and take control of the demon's powers, I would turn Dac into the vampire before the curse took over and control it. But Dac blamed me for making him the vampire and ran away. The rest, you know."

"And you still want to save him, even after what he did to you?"

"He is my brother, after all. Would you kill a family member?"

"I suppose not, but none of my family members are plagued with an evil curse."

"Fair enough. However, as you've seen, Dac doesn't want to be evil, and the real threat now is not the curse but Alex."

"So, what's the plan?"

"We're going to lure Alex out of hiding by using your connection to Nikolai as bait." Luca stood up and patted Jace on the shoulder. "I'll return tomorrow to discuss things further."

The lights flickered off, and Jace jumped up from his seat. His heart raced, and his mind felt hazy yet alert all at once as if being startled awake from a deep sleep. He raced to flip on the light switch. Luca was long gone. His house was quiet. The hawthorn still remained hanging in all the doorways and windows. The smell of essential oils still surrounded him. He checked his neck in the bathroom mirror, no new bite marks. He let out a comforting sigh. At least for now, he was safe.

Nine

Dac sat at his friend's bedside. The others had not woken yet and therefore did not know he had returned home. He timed his arrival back to Aura City so that he could spend some time alone with Nikolai before Emmaline, Harper, or Quentin woke up. He did not know what type of state he would find his old friend in, but he hadn't expected what he found.

Nikolai lay on his bed. An IV was attached to his arm, pumping blood into his veins. His eyelids remained closed without any form of movement underneath them. His vampiric pale skin had taken on a bluish-grey color. Even with the blood he was receiving, he still looked like the dead. Dac stared at his comatose friends, searching for any signs of life still in him.

"I'm so sorry, friend," Dac whispered. "But I promise I will protect you this time."

"Protect him from what?" A harsh voice asked from the doorway. "What have you done this time?"

Dac's head shot up to see Quentin standing in the doorway. He appeared as a dark ghostly shadow. His arms were folded across his chest. The scar across his face was barely visible, and his eyes glowed a yellow hue in his non-human form. "Quentin," Dac said as he stood from his chair. "Let's talk outside."

Quentin shifted from the doorway into the hall. Dac followed, gently closing the door behind him. "My brother came to see me the other night," Dac began. "He tells me Alex is missing, and the only one who has had any contact with him is Una, and she obviously isn't telling anyone where Alex is. He says Alex is still a threat."

"And now you suddenly trust your brother?" Quentin didn't even try to hide his disdain; his voice kept low and bitter.

"No, I'm sure he'll want something in return, and I'm almost certain he's done something to mess with my mind, but...."

"Mess with your mind how?" Quentin interrupted.

"That doesn't matter. Right now, the real threat is Alex."

"Alex isn't as powerful as he thinks. It's clear he has none of your brother's blood in him. And if he is hiding from Luca, it is clear that he has no loyalty to him either." Quentin pointed out.

"But he is very cunning, and his lack of loyalty makes him that much more dangerous." Dac pointed out just as the sound of footsteps came from down the hall.

"Dac!" Emmaline exclaimed as she ran into Dac's arms, the same as she had done when Quentin had returned after Luca had taken him. Dac welcomed her embrace, stroking her long red hair. "I'm so happy you're home," she said as she pulled away.

Dac smiled down at her. "Is Harper in her room?" He asked.

"No, she's gone out for the night already. She spends most nights away from the house, coming in right before sunup. I think it's hard for her to be here with Nikolai still injured and you being gone. But she'll be so happy to find out you're home. I know it." Despite everything, Emmaline always managed to keep a positive outlook on things. Dac wondered how she managed to remain so innocent throughout all she had been through in her life.

"That's understandable. I'll just see her later. But it was a rough trip back from Noxwood. I think I'll go to my room and rest for a while." He smiled at Emmaline while giving Quentin a sideways glance, then walked away towards his room.

Dac stepped into his bedroom. It was cool and dark as usual. Without turning on the lights, he made his way over to the king-size bed and slid underneath the plush comforter laying his head comfortably on the soft pillows. He closed his eyes as the melody of the music box played in his head, and he could hear little Sophia's laughter as if he were still in Noxwood, standing outside her window. What was this connection to the young girl, this child? He had to figure it out. Every time he thought of her, it reminded him of his first human kill, the young boy, who also was only a child. Was that the connection? Was the craving driving him mad, or was this Luca trying to convert him into a killer like himself. Luca liked to call it survival, but he called it murder. Dac had suppressed these instincts for so long, he was not about to give in to them now.

Unable to rest as he had hoped to do, Dac decided to go for a walk. Before leaving the house, he stopped by the kitchen at the warming vault where they kept the blood donations. He pulled out a jar of the blood and poured it into a glass. He drank the thick red substance in one gulp and wiped his mouth on a dish towel lying on the countertop. He tossed the towel back on the counter and walked out the back door into the warm night.

As he rounded the front side of the house, he noticed a shadow coming silently up the walkway. Upon further inspection, he realized it was Harper. She was returning home from wherever she had been earlier that night. He called out her name. She glanced around but then quickly ran to the front door. He called her name again before she was able to open the door. She turned her head in his direction, the light of the front entryway illuminating her face. She pretended as though she didn't see him and rushed into the house. Dac decided to nix his walk and followed Harper inside. It wasn't just that she ran from him that troubled Dac, but the coloring on her lips. When the light hit Harper's face, Dac noticed the red stain of blood on her lips.

As he stepped into the front door after Harper, he heard the wall to the stairwell that led to their rooms open and close. She was desperate to get away from him. He quickly followed after her calling her name once more. She ran down the hall, reaching her room without looking back at him. He knocked on her door. When she didn't answer, he called out to her again, banging his fist harder against the door until she finally answered. She stood with her hand clasped on the doorknob, blocking the entrance to her room.

"Dac, when did you get back?" She asked, trying to feign surprise. She had tried to cover the bloodstain on her lips with a muted lip gloss, and she had changed her clothes.

"Where were you tonight?" He asked, not bothering to answer her question.

"I was out for a walk. I like to get out and get some fresh air now and then. No reason to stay hidden inside here all night." Her voice was shaky, and he could tell she was hiding something.

"Emmaline said you go out every night and don't come back until sunup."

"She exaggerates. It's not like that. I just like to go to Aura Springs to my spot near the beach just as I've always done."

Still standing on the other side of her doorway, Dac placed his fingers under her chin, gently lifting her face to meet his eye. "How are you?" he asked, deciding to take a gentler approach with her. "I'm sorry I stayed away so long."

"I'm fine," she said as she turned her head away. Dac leaned into her sliding his hand down her back, but she pulled away from him.

"Ok then. Well, have a good night." He turned away and stomped back down the hall. Harper was definitely hiding something. She had never backed away from him like that. Who was she after this time, and what kind of trouble would it bring, he wondered? Whoever it was, he didn't have the time or mental energy to focus on it. He had to find Alex before Alex came after Nikolai again. Nikolai was far too vulnerable.

HARPER CLOSED THE DOOR to her room. She sighed with relief after Dac walked away. That was too close. He probably suspected something off with her, but he wouldn't know what she had done. What would he do if he knew she was out there feeding off of humans? The monster she had become sickened even herself. She could only imagine how Dac would react. Would he do to her what he had done to his own brother? Probably worse, she thought.

She glanced at the dagger sitting on her vanity table and was thankful Dac hadn't tried to enter her room and that he left as soon as she pushed away from him. It hurt her to reject him in that way. She missed him and the closeness they once shared. She wished things could go back to how they were before, but she was different now, and he wouldn't understand. Maybe it was time for her to move out of the house. She didn't fit in here. Perhaps she never had. She loved them all, they had taken care of her, but she always felt like an outsider. She was nothing more than a reminder, a replica, of Nikolai's dead wife. Except his wife wasn't even dead. Una was a vampire like the rest of them, and she nearly killed Nikolai. How could Harper stick around after all that had recently happened? She would only be a reminder of that trauma.

She sat at her vanity, resting her chin in her hands. Her reflection stared back at her revealing the savage creature behind the pretty facade. Red-orange speckles flickered within the greens of her eyes. The fangs that grew from her gums were stilled stained with blood. The nails on her fingertips grew out like talons. And the blood that ran through her veins, coloring her pale flesh, was not even hers. It belonged to her latest victim. In fact, nothing in the picture in front of her felt like hers. The Harper looking back at her now was not the Harper she had once known.

"You are a powerful vampire. You are a killer," Those were the words Luca had spoken to her the first night they met. *You are a killer.* The words repeated in her head over and over now as she stared at herself in the mirror. "He's right. Accept who you are," Alex had said to her.

I'm not a killer! I'm not a killer! She silently screamed. But she was. Her bloodstained fangs exposing themselves in her reflection proved just that.

The light of the chandelier reflected off the steal of the dagger next to her elbow. Her eyes gazed at the twinkling light in the metal blade. She reached over, grabbing the handle. With the cold, sharp edge of the knife pressed firmly against her skin, she swiftly swiped the blade across her throat. The blood splattered onto the vanity and mirror. Red and black liquid poured down her throat out of the gaping wound she had just created, soaking her skin and clothes. The dagger fell to the ground with a clank. Her vision blurred as colors of silver, red, and black circled around her and her eyelids closed. Her body slumped out of the chair and onto the floor.

"Harper!" She heard Cloe's voice scream out in the darkness. "No! Harper, what have you done?" But it wasn't Cloe. It was Emmaline's voice she was hearing. Emmaline had come into her room. She hadn't even heard her knock, but she was there. She could feel the warmth of the cloth being pressed against her throat, and she winced at the raw, burning sting of pain. Emmaline's voice echoed against the walls as she called out for Dac and Quentin. Within minutes Harper heard Quentin's voice. "What happened?" She heard him ask, and she sensed Dac enter the room shortly after. She seemed to be somewhere between consciousness and unconsciousness. The voices around her seemed far away though she could sense them nearby. The feeling in her body was fading to numbness. The darkness was welcoming as the voices in her head slowly faded away.

Ten

The blood spilled from her neck, soaking her skin and hair. The room was dark. A voice called out, "Harper! No!" It was Cloe's voice. No, that couldn't be right. He looked around, but all he could see was total darkness. There was no one there. He was alone, standing in the void. His body felt weightless as the floor dropped beneath him. His heart sank to the pit of his stomach. He stretched his arms out, reaching for anything to grab onto as he fell into nothingness.

Jace jolted awake. His palms felt sweaty, and he felt sick to his stomach. He sat up in his bed. Outside the window, the sky was still dark, but he could see the dawn creeping up. He laid his head back down on the pillow pulling in a deep breath. He counted to ten and exhaled. After a few more breathes like this, his heart rate finally returned to a normal beat. Staring up at the ceiling, it was evident that falling back to sleep wasn't an option, so he managed to pull himself out of bed, walk to the kitchen and make some coffee.

Sitting at his kitchen table, he stared into his coffee cup, reimagining the dream that had awoken him. It didn't make any sense. Had something happened to Harper? Why would Cloe be screaming Harper's name? Cloe was dead. But dreams weren't supposed to make sense, were they? That's the thing about dreams. They were just jumbled images your mind played back to you in your sleep. They were meaningless. Except he still couldn't shake the feeling his dreams lately were trying to tell him something. It was as if he had different parts of the puzzle, but none of them fit together. If only he could remember more than just bits and pieces.

The hours passed by with him barely noticing. When he finally looked at his phone, he saw a missed call and text from Sarah. She messaged that she'd be by in the afternoon to pick him up. They would be taking another trip to her great-grandmother's house. It was urgent. He looked at the text again and then the time. Luca had told him to stay away from Sarah. That was part of their deal. But he didn't know if he could even trust Luca. Plus, she was already involved, whether Luca liked it or not. Maybe he could find a way to work with both of them without the other knowing. He would figure out exactly how to pull that off later. For now, he messaged Sarah back, telling her to come now. It was already late in the morning. If they were going to make it to her grandmother's place and back before nightfall, they would need to leave sooner rather than later.

He had just finished washing up and dressing when he heard the knock on the door. He snatched his wallet and keys off the counter and met Sarah outside. They mainly drove in silence the entire trip to Sarah's grandmother, neither having much to say. Once they arrived, it was Sarah's grandmother who answered the door, not her caretaker. She quickly ushered them into the house, and they followed her into the same sitting room they had met in the last time they were there.

"Marie is dead," Brigid said, getting straight to the point as usual.

"Marie?" Sarah questioned.

"My nurse. She was found murdered last night in Aura City. I'm sure you can guess what happened." The bitterness ran deep in Brigid's words. She was very clearly blaming Marie's death on Sarah's and Jace's last visit.

"Alex," Jace blurted out without thinking. Both Sarah and her grandmother looked at him, puzzled. Jace cleared his throat and continued. "Luca was at my house the other night." He bowed his head and lowered his voice as he spoke as if someone nearby might hear him revealing the secret.

"The brother of the seventh son," Brigid interrupted.

"Yes. Him." Jace continued. "Alex is the reason he survived his brother's attack, but Alex has been out for revenge against his father, Nikolai. He's the vampire Luca's brother made. Only now Alex has disappeared, and being as he is a threat to Luca's brother, and Luca is aware of my acquaintance with him, he has asked me for help."

"What exactly does he want you to do?" Sarah asked.

"He offered me a deal. In exchange for helping lure Alex out of hiding, he would help me find Cloe's killer." Jace replied. "Oh, and I am supposed to stop working with you, Sarah." Jace knew he shouldn't be saying any of this. He knew by telling them they could both be put in danger, but in light of the current news, he felt he had no choice. Keeping secrets from Cloe got her killed. Maybe if he would have told her about Harper and the vampires, she could have defended herself. He never thought one of them would find her. And now Brigid's nurse was dead. Obviously killed by a vampire, or Brigid wouldn't have called them here, he had to speak up. He had to tell them both of Luca's plan before they both ended up dead too.

"And you took the deal, Jace? Why didn't you tell me?" Sarah was understandably shocked and a little bit concerned.

"Well, I didn't really have a choice. Luca basically said he would kill me otherwise."

"I suppose you had no other choice then," Brigid said. Sarah nodded in agreement though Jace could see the irritation in her face. "Anyway. Sarah, I will be coming back to Aura Springs and staying with you. That is why I called you two over here today."

"Do you really think that's the safest thing to do right now?" Sarah asked.

"It's the only thing to do. You two will need me more now than before."

"But..." Sarah started to pretest, but her grandmother interrupted her before she could say anything further.

"I'm not as fragile as you think. And you will need my knowledge of these vampires now that they are aware of your plans. Young man," Brigid turned towards Jace. "You will work with this vampire, Luca, as agreed. I will mix you a stronger potion once we get back to Sarah's that will help to conceal your thoughts from the vampire. But you must be extremely careful not to let on that we are all still working together." Jace could still hear the hostility coming from Brigid, which made him wonder about her intentions. Why was she so suddenly determined to help them when just the other day she had so blatantly refused?

"Understood." Jace shook his head even though he knew Brigid probably couldn't see him. He wondered to himself if she had any sight at all or if it was total darkness behind her eyes. He hardly knew her and nothing of her condition, so he was too embarrassed to ask.

"Now, we must get moving if we are to get back before sundown. We don't want to take any chances of being seen together. The vampire will be watching Jace once he awakens." Brigid started making her way towards the door.

Jace gathered up Brigid's suitcase that was waiting by the front entrance. Sarah helped her grandmother to the car as Jace put her things into the trunk. Not long after, they were back in Aura Springs.

Sarah dropped Jace off at his house. He offered to go back to Sarah's to help get her grandmother settled in, but they refused. Brigid said it was best they were not around each other after the sun began its descent. Instead, they all agreed to meet early the next morning. Jace watched as Sarah pulled away and drove off. He entered his house and immediately looked for the cream Brigid had given him at their first meeting. He rubbed the cream on his temples, neck, and wrists. He sat on his couch, turned on the tv, and waited for the night to come.

The hard knock on the door roused Jace from his daydream. As expected, Luca was standing on the other side of the threshold. Jace stepped aside and motioned for Luca to enter. Tonight, they sat in the kitchen. Jace poured himself a cup of coffee and offered one to Luca, who refused. "Oh right, of course," Jace said in reply. He glanced at the bottle of whiskey that sat on the countertop next to the coffee pot. He opened it and added a little to his coffee. Once Jace finally settled down at the table, Luca began to speak.

"Normally, your protections would make me distrust you, but for the sake of our mission, I suppose they are necessary," Luca said of the cream Jace used to block Luca from his thoughts and the oils Jace kept in his pocket and wore around his neck.

"But don't you distrust me anyway?" Maybe it was the whiskey, but he was feeling a little more relaxed tonight.

"Maybe it was due to your friendship with Harper, but you were loyal to my brother, so I'll take my chances."

"Plus, you'll kill me if I betray you."

"Precisely. Now, let's get down to business. My brother is back in town, so my guess would be Alex is not far behind."

"Isn't that what we want, though?"

"Yes, but we must be prepared. And we must get to Alex before he gets to Dac and Nikolai. My brother is far too distracted right now. He is not himself." There was a flash of concern on Luca's face. An expression that Jace hadn't noticed before, but he was beginning to believe maybe Luca did actually care about his brother.

"So, what's the plan? What do you want me to do?"

"You will first lure Alex to you with your thoughts, inviting him to seek you out. Of course, you will need to wipe yourself clean of your protective cream. He will need to hear you calling to him but be careful to keep your mind clear of any thoughts that will give away your true intentions. Once he arrives, convince him you are on his side and that you have turned against Harper, Dac, and the others. Get him to trust you. It won't be hard. He can be cunning, but he is driven by anger which at times can make him careless. Strike a deal with him similar to the one you have with me. He'll be expecting you to want something in return for helping him. Once he agrees to work with you, which I know he will, start wearing your cream again. You will not want him accessing your mind. He will want to meet with you at his location. Once he tells you where that is, contact me at this number, and we'll discuss what to do next." Luca handed Jace a slip of paper with a phone number on it.

"Should I call or text this number?" Jace asked, looking at the paper.

"A simple text will do. I will meet you back here once I receive your message."

"So, I won't hear from you again until then?"

"That's correct. Alex will be watching you until he feels certain you're trustworthy. We can't risk him seeing us together. It will make him suspicious."

"But I thought you two were friends?"

"Well, when his little plan last winter didn't go his way and his true intentions were revealed, things changed. I may owe him for saving my life, but his reasons for doing so were misleading."

"What were his true intentions? I thought he just wanted revenge against his father."

"That is true, but he also blamed my brother and me for the part we played in his mother's turning and him growing up an orphan. He befriended me because he needed my strength and power, but, in the end, he expected Dac and I to destroy each other."

"I see."

"I must go now. Tonight, get your story together. Tomorrow call for Alex."

As usual, Luca left so quickly that Jace did not see him go. If it had not been for the door nearly slamming shut, he would have thought Luca was still in the house somewhere. Still, he searched the house, making sure Luca was, in fact, gone. Then he texted Sarah to confirm their meeting for the following day and spent the rest of the night deciding what he would say to Alex if and when he finally came face to face with the vengeful vampire.

Eleven

Sarah and her grandmother had shown up at Jace's house early the next morning. Jace poured coffee for each of them, and they all settled around the kitchen table. He told them about his visit from Luca the night before and the plan Luca had for him to contact Alex. Sarah and Brigid both agreed it could be beneficial for all if Jace were able to convince Alex he was on his side, although Brigid had another request. She wanted Jace to find the dagger that was used to injure Luca. They knew Harper had it with her when she had been taken by Luca last winter and that Alex was going to use it against his father. Chances were, Alex still had the dagger. "What if he doesn't?" Jace asked, knowing it was possible that someone else had picked it up in the battle.

"I agree it could be back with the others, but maybe you can use your past acquaintance with them to find out," Brigid suggested.

"Except that Luca will be watching the house." Jace reminded her.

They agreed for now that Jace would find out if Alex still had the dagger, and if not, they would later come up with another plan. They also agreed they would meet on a regular basis to discuss Jace's progress with Alex and whatever he found out from the vampire, and what next steps Luca had planned for him. From there, they would decide their next steps. At the moment, however, Luca's plan was the best way for them to gain access to these vampires.

Once Sarah and her grandmother left, Jace tried to get on with his day as normal, except nothing about his days had been normal in months. He messaged Alan to check in on work and let him know he would be working from home for a while. Sarah had returned briefly with a few things she said Jace would need for successfully breaking into Alex's thoughts since he wasn't connected to him through a bite. Her grandmother had said these things would guarantee Alex heard him. Without them, it could take days for Alex to detect him, especially if he weren't aware of him actively seeking him out.

"But I thought they could sense when humans were hunting them?" Jace had asked her.

"They can sense when we are nearby, yes. But when you are trying to reach out from a distance, they may not hear you." Sarah had explained before she left out the door.

Jace looked through the box as he went over in his head the conversation with Brigid from earlier that morning. He wondered why she was suddenly eager to help and why she was so concerned with that dagger. What was so important about it? He thought the death of her nurse would have scarred her further from talking about the vampires, but it seemed to spark something in her. It appeared it had brought out the vampire hunter she had been as a young woman. He began to wonder what her story was. How had she started hunting vampires, and what made her stop?

As the sun began its descent for the evening, Jace washed the protection cream off his skin and readied himself to contact Alex. He peered into the box Sarah had brought him earlier. Inside were two black candles and one red one. There was a vial full of a red powdery substance and a piece of paper with instructions. He dimmed the lights in his living room and set the candles on the coffee table, the two black ones at the ends and the red one in the middle forming a triangle. He lit each candle carefully. In the center of the triangle, he placed the vial of red powder.

He sat on the floor facing the table and closed his eyes. Breathing in long deep, slow breaths, he began his meditation, centering himself and clearing his mind of all his thoughts until he finally felt at peace. It was relaxing for those few moments as his body felt as though it had melted into the floor. But it was a fleeting moment as he knew it was time to call out to the vampire.

With his mind cleared of any visions of Cloe, Sarah, and her grandmother, Luca, or any other vampires, Jace began to whisper Alex's name. He said it three times as the instructions had said for him to do, and then he stated his intentions by asking Alex to come to him. Within moments an apparition appeared before him. The figure in front of him looked like the bartender at the card game last winter. He hadn't known it at the time, but the host of that game was Luca, and his team of vampires and Alex had been the one behind the bar. As the man stood before him now, he noticed his dark eyes and glimmering fanged teeth. But he wasn't really in his house. It was just an image, and as the image disappeared, a folded yellow sheet of paper appeared on the coffee table.

Jace stood up and turned the lights on. He blew out the candles and picked up the yellow paper. He unfolded it and looked at the writing. It was a message from Alex with an address telling Jace to meet him there the next night. Jace's hand started to tremble slightly. He hadn't known what to expect when he called for Alex tonight, but he hadn't expected to be invited to meet him so quickly. He tucked the paper into his jeans pocket before going into the bedroom, rubbing the protective cream all over his neck and wrists and changing into sleep clothes. The whole night had drained him. Tiredness was taking over his mind and body though he knew his sleep would be restless.

WITH LAST NIGHT ON his mind, Jace spread his protective cream once again across his neck, temples, and wrists. He pulled the necklace of oil over his head. It hung loosely around his neck. He put the additional vials of oils and a small pocketknife in his pants pocket. He wasn't certain the pocketknife was necessary or even that it would be helpful if he did find himself in a situation where he might need it, but he took it anyway.

Deciding not yet to tell Luca or Sarah, he followed the directions on the yellow paper Alex had left for him. He wanted to meet with Alex alone first without anyone else's knowledge or influence. He thought it would be better this way if he was going to gain Alex's trust as they all wanted him to do. In the end, he wasn't doing this for any of them. While they all had their own reasons, Jace's only concern was getting to Cloe's killer, and he was willing to do that by any means possible.

As he learned to do with his past encounters with vampires, he parked his car a few blocks away from his destination and walked the rest of the way. It seemed kind of stupid if he needed to make a quick getaway, but it allowed him a little more time before any vampires would hear him coming since they could sense the vibrations of the car long before they would sense him.

The area of town the directions had taken him was quiet and deserted. The neighborhood was lined with long-abandoned houses, townhomes, and storefronts. Large trees hovered over the streets blocking any light from the moon above. There were no street lamps to light the way while he walked. He used the light from his phone to read the numbers on the empty buildings.

He stopped in front of what appeared to be an abandoned church. Ivy vines clung to the Romanesque-styled building. The iron gates that once protected the front doors were rusted and falling off their hinges. He looked down at the address written on the paper in his hand, then back up at the numbers inscribed on the metal plague that hung loosely off the gate. This had to be the place.

As he approached, one of the gates swung open. He took a deep breath and walked across the grass-covered walkway. When he reached the entrance of the building, he casually stepped through the arched doorway. He tried his best to appear unafraid though inside his heart was pounding. The murky, humid air inside the building, on top of his anxiety, made it hard to breathe. A flicker of light like two glowing eyes in the darkness flashed in front of him but quickly disappeared. A cool breeze caused him to shiver despite the warm temperatures.

"Hello!" Jace called out. When no one answered, he stepped further into the church. The rubble of fallen plaster and other debris crunched beneath his feet. With every breath, dust entered his lungs. His hands and knees were shaking, although he somehow managed to keep himself steady and upright. He wandered around the pitch-dark room in search of the vampire who invited him here. "Alex?" He called again. Still, no one answered, but he could feel the presence of someone or something nearby.

A rustling sound came from the corner of the room. Jace turned his head to see the flicker of yellow eyes glowing in the dark. The creature hissed. It was only a cat, Jace realized as it darted away. He let out a short breath. He moved further up the nave of the church to the sanctuary. He stepped up closer to the alter, then turned to open the door to his left, which appeared to lead to the sacristy. The whole place seemed empty, aside from the scattered wreckage of the old building.

Just as he was about to give up, turn around and leave this place, a cold hand reached out and grabbed his shoulder. His heart skipped a beat as he froze in place. The hand that held him turned him around so he was facing the vampire that now had him in its grasp. The one standing in front of him was not who he had expected. It was not Alex. It was a woman. Her long black hair reflected the moonlight that shined through the broken stained-glass window. Her pale face resembled Harper's, but no, she was not Harper.

"Did you really think I would let you trap my son, vampire hunter?" Her voice was penetrating and powerful. And although she stood around Jace's same height, it seemed as though she towered over him.

"Your son?" Jace tried his best not to let his voice crack though he felt it might. "Ah, you must be Una." He said, realizing who she was. "I swear I wasn't trying to trap him. I just wanted to ask for his help." Jace pleaded with her.

"Ha. Do not think you can trick me, vampire hunter." She gripped his shoulder tighter, digging her sharp nails into his skin.

Jace swallowed hard before answering. "I promise I'm not trying to trick you. And please stop calling me vampire hunter. I'm not a vampire hunter." He pleaded with her.

"Maybe I need to remind you of how I removed Harper's blood from you and replaced it with mine. You forget I am a part of your mind now and forever." She replied, reminding him of when she tricked him into thinking she was Harper.

"That was you in her room that night? You were the one who rushed me out of the house. That wasn't Harper. You bit me that night. That's why I didn't get any images from her after that." Jace pulled away from her, surprised she let him go.

"That's right. See, you do remember."

"But I can see her now."

"Can you now?" She raised an eyebrow.

"Yes, well, maybe. I don't know. They're just dreams. Maybe it's nothing?" Jace rubbed his hands across his face as he paced back and forth, though never taking his eyes off the vampire. He felt himself becoming flustered.

"Ah, yes, your little dreams you try to hide when you rub your cream across your skin." She knew of his dreams and the cream he had been using. Did she know what the dreams meant?

"You can see my dreams?"

"Well, I could until, as I said, you used your creams to block me from your mind."

"It wasn't you. Well, I didn't know it was you. I just want all the vampires out of mind." His courage was faltering. He wondered if she sensed it.

"You want more than that. Why else would you be looking for Alex? You want the vampire that killed your little girlfriend. Don't you?" She leaned in close to him. Her breath was cold against his face. She sensed his fear, and she enjoyed it.

"Ok. Yes, I'll admit I want to know who killed Cloe."

"And you want to destroy them, don't you, vampire hunter?"

"Yes!" Jace yelled in frustration. "I want to destroy them. When I found that I couldn't get help from Harper and the others. The ones I thought were my friends. I thought I could get help from Alex in exchange for...."

"In exchange for what?" Una interrupted, grabbing hold of Jace's throat.

"In exchange for Nikolai," Jace answered though her tight grip made it hard for him to speak.

"I see," Una said as she let go of Jace and circled around him. "So, you are willing to betray your friends to get justice for your love?"

"They are no longer my friends. Perhaps they never were." Jace said solemnly.

"Perhaps," Una said, turning her eyes back to Jace.

"So, do we have a deal? Will you and Alex help me?" Jace asked.

"I'll think about it." She answered. "In the meantime, be careful, vampire hunter. You do not know what type of trouble you are seeking."

In a flash, she was gone, and Jace was left alone again in the empty church. His eyelids suddenly felt heavy, and his shoulders ached as if from a lack of sleep. He felt himself wishing for water as his mouth became dry. He tried to blink away the black spots forming in front of his eyes. His body became weak, and the room began to slowly spin. Then before he knew what had happened, he sunk down onto the ground into a state of unconsciousness.

Twelve

"What is he doing here?"

"I had to bring him somewhere. Couldn't just leave him there. What do you want to do with him?"

"I don't know."

"I told you the human couldn't be trusted."

"But he helped us out the last time."

"And now he's seeking out the enemy."

"What exactly did you hear him say?"

"That he would trade Nikolai for Alex's help."

"That doesn't make any sense. How would he even expect to do that?"

"I don't know. He must have help from somewhere. I've removed all his trinkets from his neck and the oils from his pockets, so he'll have no protections from us once he wakes up. That is if you want him to wake up."

"Good idea. Thank you. Yes, we'll want him to wake up. Let's get all the info we can get from him first. Then we can decide what to do with him. In the meantime, lock him in an empty room downstairs, then go sit with Nikolai. He's still not any better. I'll go talk to Harper and Emmaline."

Quentin grabbed Jace's comatose body and advanced down the stairs. Dac sent messages to both Harper and Emmaline to meet him upstairs in his office rather than searching the house for them. He sat at his desk while he waited. Harper was the first to arrive. Dac felt a pang of sorrow and pity when he noticed the white bandage still wrapped around her neck. When his eyes met hers, she averted her gaze. This was the first time he had seen her since he had run into her room after hearing Emmaline calling for help, only to find Emmaline on the floor, holding a cloth over Harper's throat to stop the blood from flowing out of the wound she had inflicted on herself. Dac desperately wanted to talk to Harper about whatever was going on with her. He wondered what would cause her to do such a thing. When he tried to speak to her that night, she had run away from him. She had pushed him away, so he had left her alone. He could see she was struggling, but he hadn't realized how much. Unfortunately, now wasn't the time to talk about it. Maybe he would ask her to stick around after he spoke to her and Emmaline about Jace. But right now, they had a new threat, and he had to prepare the both of them.

It wasn't long before Emmaline joined them in Dac's office. She sat down in the chair next to Harper and put one hand on top of one of Harper's as a gesture of comfort. Neither knew yet why Dac wanted to speak with them. He spoke softly as he explained that Quentin had seen Jace walking into an abandoned church. He felt concerned, so he followed him inside. That's when he realized Jace was there to meet Una. Quentin had lingered long enough to hear Jace proposition Una for help. Once it was safe and Una had gone, Quentin drained Jace's energy and brought him back to the house, where he was now locked inside one of the rooms downstairs. Dac explained how this now made Jace a threat to their existence. Dac hadn't, however, expected the look of guilt he saw cross Emmaline's face.

"What is it?" he asked when Emmaline hadn't volunteered any information.

"Jace was here the other night," she said softly. "He asked for my help to find out who killed his fiancée. He says it was a vampire." Harper let out a small gasp. They both looked at her then Emmaline went on, "I told him I couldn't help and just to move on. I can't help feeling like this is somewhat my fault, but I never thought he would go asking for help from some other vampire. Especially one of them. I mean, wouldn't it be likely it was one of them anyway? They probably know he had helped us before. That was probably their retaliation."

"This isn't your fault, although you're probably right. And now they're going to use his grief to try to get to Nikolai and finish what they started. We can't let that happen." Dac replied to Emmaline. He noticed that Harper had stayed quiet throughout the entire conversation. He knew this news would be hard for her to hear. Harper and Jace had been close friends. She wouldn't want to believe her friend, someone she trusted with her life, would now be her enemy. But maybe it was just the wound on her throat that kept her from speaking.

He tried his best to reassure them both that they would figure things out after he had a chance to speak with Jace. He told Emmaline she could leave but asked Harper to stay back. He wanted an opportunity to talk to her alone.

"I'm worried about you." He said to Harper.

"Worried about me?" She scoffed. "It wasn't too long along that you threatened me, said that you'd destroy me. No need to be worried about me now." Before he could respond, Harper had disappeared out the door and down the hall.

He stood in the doorway to his office and let out a deep sigh. She was right to be mad at him, but he had to keep everyone protected. That was his duty as head of this family that he created, even if he hadn't been doing such a great job of that lately.

THERE WAS THE CLICKING sound of a lock and the squeak of a door being opened. A tiny yellow light penetrated the darkness behind his closed eyelids. The ground, hard and cold beneath him, felt like stone. His body twisted and he wrapped his arms around his waist as the hardened sole of a boot made contact with his side. He heard the faint words of a familiar voice. "Wake up," the voice had said. Who was the person that belonged to this voice? He knew it though he could not place its owner. Another kick from the boot and a soft whimper escaped his lips. His eyelids fluttered. He tried unsuccessfully to open his eyes and peel himself off of the floor. His body felt weak and ached all over. What happened, and where was he?

"Wake up." The voice demanded.

Jace still struggled to open his eyes. The yellow light grew slightly brighter. The man in the room held up a lantern, and Jace could finally see his face. He rubbed his eyes with his fist and lazily sat upright. "Where am I?" He asked, suddenly realizing who was in front of him, although he didn't relax, sensing he was in danger from the familiar vampire. His voice was raspy, and he knew Dac could sense his fear.

Dac crouched down in front of him, resting the lantern on the floor. He put a hand on Jace's shoulder. Jace's muscles instantly tensed up, and his arm moved as he reached for his pocket. "Don't bother," Dac said. His voice held firm as it had the very first night Jace had come to the vampire house. "Your trinkets and oils have been removed."

"What happened? Why am I here?"

"You are here because you seek to make deals with the enemy."

"It is not what you think." Jace wanted to plead with him, but he knew he couldn't reveal the plan. He could only hope Dac would be understanding. Though by the looks of things at the moment, that didn't seem likely.

"Then tell me, what is it?"

"I – I can't. But you must believe me. I swear..." Jace stuttered, tripping over his words, trying to find the right things to say without saying too much. But his mind still felt clouded, making his attempt to explain himself unsuccessful.

"I must do nothing." Dac stood up, glaring down at Jace. Frustration and disdain for a person he once trusted written across his face. "If you can't tell me what you were doing making deals with Una, then you will rot here until I decide what to do with you." He picked up the lantern and turned to leave the room.

"Please..." Jace began to protest. Dac turned around to face him, but Jace would explain himself no further.

"I no longer drink directly from humans, but I may just make an exception for you. You may want to rethink where your loyalties lie." Dac's lips drew back, revealing his large, fanged teeth. The yellow light of the lantern cast a shadow across his face. Jace locked eyes with Dac as the vampire's gaze bore down at him with evil intent. He felt his body quiver with fear, his shoulders hunched over, and his hands trembled. Then Dac stepped out of the room, locking the door behind him, leaving Jace alone in his solitary prison.

Thirteen

Harper stood outside the door listening to Dac speaking with Jace. She needed to know what Jace knew, but he wasn't saying anything. Why wouldn't he just tell Dac what was going on? She heard Dac approach the door, and she ducked around the corner. She watched as he stepped out of the room and descended down the long corridor, probably to check on Nikolai. Once she was confident all was clear, she wandered over to the door. She reached above the door frame, where she saw Dac place the key, and she unlocked to door to Jace's room.

Jace was sitting curled up on the floor in the far corner of the room, his knees tucked to his chest, his arms wrapped around his legs and his head hung low. He gasped when he heard the door open. Realizing that he couldn't see her in the pitch-dark room, Harper wished she had thought to bring a flashlight. She had sensed his fear and felt terrible for startling him.

"It's ok," she said, trying to set him at ease. "It's me, Harper."

"Did your friend send you in here to try to get me to tell you what I've been up to?" Jace asked.

Harper inched closer to her friend. She sat on the floor next to him with her back against the wall. "No," She answered. "But why won't you tell him?"

"I can't. I gave my word that I wouldn't say anything."

"But Dac will kill you if you don't."

83

"And the other will kill me if I do." There was no way out of this situation. It was utterly hopeless. He had failed Cloe. If he could have burrowed himself any deeper into the wall, he would have.

"I see," Harper said. She reached her arm around her old friend's shoulder. The thumping of his heart as it pulsed with every beat that vibrated in her ears. The scent of his human blood crept into her nostrils, tempting her vampiric instincts. Her own heart skipped a beat and her mouth watered as she recalled the taste of his blood. She pushed down her craving and rested her head against his, cradling him in a friendly embrace.

Neither of them knew how long they had stayed like that. The silence between them was comfortable and familiar. Harper didn't bother to acknowledge the tears she felt drip from Jace's eyes. His pain was her fault. If she hadn't dragged him into helping her, he and Cloe would still be living a happy life together.

"Harper, can you get me out of here?" Jace finally asked, breaking the silence between them.

"Dac and I aren't on such great terms these days. I'll ask Emmaline to talk to him. I know she really likes you. I'm sure she can convince Dac you aren't a threat. I know you're not. If she can't, I'll figure out a way to sneak you out of here. I'll come back for you. For now, I should go before Dac comes back. He told us not to come in here."

"And yet you did anyway."

"Of course, I did. You're one of my closest friends Jace. I promise I won't let anything bad happen to you." Harper hugged her friend before getting up from the floor.

"I'm not sure you can really promise that, but thank you," He wiped the tears from his face, a small amount of hope coming back to him.

"I'll be back soon," Harper said as she left the room, locking the door behind her. She placed the key back in its spot above the door frame and made her way quickly upstairs to the main floor.

Harper wandered into the kitchen. She grabbed a glass from the cabinet and a vial of blood from the hidden vault. The vault kept the blood warm. The thick red liquid quenched her thirst as it slid down her throat, but it did not temper her lust for the human soul. But there was something that came in a close second, she thought when she looked down at the veins in her wrists.

As she sat there sipping the remnants of blood from her glass, she caught a glimpse of a shadow passing by the window. She got up from the stool she was seated on and rushed to the window. She pulled back the bamboo blinds, but she saw nothing outside. Cautiously she opened the kitchen door and peeked her head outside, checking in all directions. The night seemed quiet as usual. It showed no evidence of anyone being nearby. At that moment, the floorboards creaked above her from heavy footsteps. No vampire would make a sound. Those footsteps were human.

Harper climbed the steps two at a time, hoping to catch whoever was upstairs unaware. When she reached the second floor, she saw no one in the hallway, but she did notice a light on in Dac's office. Whoever was here wasn't too worried about being discreet. She crept silently down the hall until she reached Dac's office door. Just as she was about to enter the room, she heard voices and paused. She rested her back against the wall keeping herself out of sight so she could listen. The voices she heard belonged to Dac and Charlotte, the daytime housekeeper. But why did Dac call her over here at night, and why would he be speaking to her in person. He had never done such a thing the entire time Harper had lived in the house with them. He had always communicated with any human helpers over the phone, whether it be a voice call or a text. She had only ever seen Charlotte on a rare occasion as it was customary for Charlotte to leave before sunset.

They spoke in hushed tones, though with her vampiric senses, she should have been able to hear them. Whatever they were talking about, Dac must have wanted to keep it secret, and he must have sensed her nearby because the only thing she could hear was static. The white noise crackled in her eardrums. The sound intensified causing her head to ache. She pressed her index finger to her ear, rubbing it as she walked away.

She roamed the house in search of Emmaline or Quentin but found neither of them. Figuring one of them at least would be with Nikolai, she made her way to his room, but when she got there, she was surprised to see him alone. There was no one watching over him. She stepped into the room and sat in the chair beside his bed. He looked peaceful except for the IV that was still feeding blood into his veins. This was the first time Harper had been alone with Nikolai since they had brought him home.

She wanted to say something to him, but no words that came to mind could express the pain, guilt, and sorrow that she felt. He was more than just the one who made her a vampire, he was her friend, her family, and she had failed and betrayed him. She sat staring at Nikolai thinking of all the times he had comforted her throughout the years she had been with them. They connected on a different level than she had with any of the others, including Dac. Maybe it was because he was the one who made her, but she felt it was something more profound than that. Perhaps because she was a descendant of Una even though neither of them had known that until recently. Whatever it was, she wasn't ready to lose him or that connection. She laid her head lightly on his chest. The tears she had been holding in began to fall when suddenly she felt a hand stroke her hair. She raised her head slightly, not expecting what she saw. Nikolai was awake.

"I NEED THE TWO OF YOU to go out to Noxwood as soon as possible, tomorrow morning if you can," Dac said to both Charlotte and Garrett, who sat facing the vampire in this rare face-to-face meeting. Charlotte had been the housekeeper for years, and Garrett was employed at the blood donation center and delivered the donations to the house every morning. Both were paid very handsomely for their discretion and proved themselves to be loyal associates of the vampire.

"To Noxwood? What for?" Charlotte asked.

"There is a young girl that lives out there. She has a music box. I need you to speak with her parents. Offer to purchase the music box from them. Then I need you to bring it back here to me. But you must be very discrete about this. No one can know about it." Dac said.

"You want us to take a music box from a little girl?" Charlotte asked again.

"I'll be giving you enough money to offer her parents that they can but ten new music boxes, but I need that one." Dac was insistent. If he was right, and that was the music box he thought it was, he needed it in his possession. And he needed to destroy it.

"But why is that specific one so important?" Charlotte demanded to know, but Dac put up a finger to silence her. He got up from his seat behind his desk and rushed towards the door. Both Charlotte and Garrett turned in their seats, but Dac motioned for them to stay still. With a flick of his hand, he swiftly yet quietly shut the door.

"I think it may be connected to something important. Now that's all I'm going to say about it." He said in a hushed yet uncompromising tone. He sat back down in his chair and opened the top drawer of the desk, pulling out a sealed envelope. He pushed the envelope towards his two associates. "Take this," he said. "Inside is the money you will offer for the music box. And here is the address to where the girl lives." He added, pointing to the yellow sticky note attached to the envelope. He instructed Charlotte and Garrett on what to say when they approached Sophia's parents about the music box. Then he pulled another envelope out of the drawer. "This is your payment and expenses for the trip. When I get the box, you'll get more. Now, wait here 5 minutes, then leave quietly. Try your best to let no one see you."

Dac left out of his office in search of Harper. He had sensed her come upstairs and needed to make sure she hadn't overheard anything, and if she had, what it was that she may have heard. The last thing he needed right now was her or anyone else asking questions. They all had enough to worry about with Alex and now Jace. They didn't need to know that, yet another threat may be out there, and with any luck, Sophia's parents had no idea the powers that the music box held. But that is why he couldn't go to them himself.

Fourteen

His arm and hand were tingling. His neck was stiff, and his head ached. His mouth and throat were dry, and his lips were cracked. There was light beyond his eyelids if he could just force them open. He peeled himself off the cold, hard floor, shook out his arm, and rubbed his neck. A lantern and tray of water and toast were placed on the floor at the other side of his windowless prison. Someone must have left it for him while he slept. How long had he slept for anyway? Was it daytime yet? He couldn't tell in this constant darkness. The vampires had taken his phone away when they locked him in this room. They were definitely less accommodating than his last stay.

His legs wobbled when he tried to stand, so instead, he crawled across the room. He drank the water straight from the steel pitcher since there was no glass. The cool liquid wet his lips, mouth, and throat, quenching his thirst. His stomach grumbled when he looked at the few pieces of buttered toast on the plate. He ate the bread taking sips of water in between bites. The thought then occurred to him that maybe whoever left the food had forgotten to lock the door. Maybe this was Harper's way of sneaking him out of here. Had she brought him food and left the door unlocked so he could make his escape? He reached out, twisting at the doorknob, but to his disappointment, the door was locked. He was still trapped, still a prisoner in this dark hell. He sunk back down to the floor, shoulders slouched in despair. He leaned his ear against the door to listen for any voices nearby. There was nothing but silence and the sound of his own heartbeat. He wondered if Harper had come up with a plan to help him escape yet. It must be morning, he thought, or she would have been back by now.

Maybe he should have just told Dac why he had met with Una and why he was looking for Alex. But Luca had warned him about telling anyone the plan or even that they were working together. Somehow Jace figured he'd have a better chance with Dac than with Luca, but now he was starting to change his mind. Whether they knew it or not, in the end, they were all on the same side. Why couldn't they just see that? Maybe he wasn't cut out for this vampire hunting thing after all. How had he gotten caught so quickly? He thought he had taken every precaution. Still, Quentin had seen and followed him, and now he was here wondering if he would live or die. And even if he somehow managed to get out of here, what would Luca do? Would he kill him just for getting caught?

That's it, he decided. If he managed to make it out of this situation, he was done with these vampires for good. To hell with it. He was going to tell Sarah and her grandmother he quit. He was ready to forget vampires ever existed. Maybe he would sell his house and move somewhere far away from here. Yea, that's what he would do. He would move away and start a whole new life someplace else. With that thought, he lay back on the hardened floor; his hands extended above him, resting under his head as he stared up at the blank ceiling.

The darkness grew around him as he rested his head against the floor. The sound of Cloe's laughter echoed off the walls. What happened to the light of the lantern? Was this a dream or a delusion? The sight of Cloe's curly brown hair cascading to her shoulders gave him comfort. The scent of her perfume surrounded him, and the warmth of her spirit engulfed his chilled skin. He sat straight up. He turned his head from side to side, following the sweet sound of her voice, searching for her in the darkness though he couldn't find her. It must be a dream, he decided, and he let his body collapse back to the ground.

Hours had passed since he had fallen asleep. He could hear voices outside his prison door. Within minutes a breeze entered the room, and he realized Quentin was standing over him. His heart dropped to the pit of his stomach when Quentin's hand reached down and snatched him up by his shoulder. Pain traced down his arm like an electrical shock. Jace stumbled over his feet as Quentin pulled him out of the room into the hall. The dim lights that lined the walls stung his eyes until they adjusted from the darkness he had become accustomed to overnight.

"Where are you taking me?" Jace asked as Quentin continued dragging him down the long corridor. Quentin didn't answer, and his cold silence made Jace shiver. They continued walking up the stairs to the main floor of the house and then up the next flight of stairs to the second floor. From there, Quentin led him to another stairwell. His grip still held firmly around Jace's upper arm.

When they reached the top of the steps, Jace noticed the heavy-looking arched double doors. Unsurprisingly Quentin opened them with ease. He pushed Jace inside. Jace stumbled but caught his balance before he hit the ground. A single small desk lamp lit the room. Swords hung from the walls. Jars filled with clear liquids sat on a shelf. Metal and wooden stakes were laid out on a table against the far wall. Jace wondered for a moment why he was brought up here, and then he noticed Dac standing there with the dagger in his hand.

Jace felt the lump grow in his throat, and he swallowed hard. Even in his panicked state, he made a mental note of the room and of the dagger. This must be where it was kept amongst the other weapons. He wondered if these were the weapons Dac and Nikolai had used all those years ago when they were hunting Luca and his coven of vampires. He'd be sure to tell Sarah and her grandmother all about this if he managed to somehow get out of here alive. Although, at the moment, he seriously doubted he would.

In an instant, Dac was standing in front of him with the blood-stained blade of the dagger resting at his throat. This must be the dagger that everyone had been talking about lately. The one Dac had once used to stab his brother. The same dagger Harper had stolen when she went after Zaine and the one Alex was going to use on Nikolai, although Quentin had stopped him, and Una stabbed him instead. Jace couldn't help but wonder what was so special about this particular dagger. Another question he would need answered if he survived this night.

Quentin was holding both of Jace's arms tightly behind his back now. Jace inhaled deeply and held his breath as Dac traced the dagger lightly across his jugular. Jace's heart was racing. Dac was staring down at his throat with glowing, lusting eyes. He curled his upper lip into a smirk revealing his sharp fangs.

"You still have a lot to learn before you can start hunting vampires. Too bad you won't live that long. I told you once before you'd need faster reflexes, vampire hunter." Dac said, referring to their very first encounter.

"And I told you, I don't want to hunt vampires." Jace managed to reply.

"But isn't that exactly what you are doing, meeting in abandoned churches, and making deals to trade one vampire for another?"

"I told you it's not what you think!"

"Then here's your last chance to explain yourself."

"I told you I can't. He'll – he'll kill me if I tell you."

"And I will kill you if you don't." Dac snarled.

Jace swallowed hard and cleared his throat, weighing his options. Quentin tightened his grip on his arms. Either way, he was a dead man, he thought. But at that moment, the door swung open behind them.

"Leave him alone, Dac." Jace heard Luca's voice say from behind him.

"What are you doing here? And what does this have to do with you?" Dac turned to his brother but kept the knife at Jace's throat.

"He's working for me. That's what. Now let him go."

Quentin looked toward Dac for instruction. Dac nodded, and Quentin released his grip on Jace and tossed him towards Luca. To Jace's surprise, Luca wasn't standing there alone. Harper was with him.

"Thank you," Harper said softly.

Dac looked at her, his eye glowing with a fiery vehemence Jace had never seen before. "And you, Harper, this is the last time you will ever betray me." He said sharply, raising the dagger above his shoulder. Jace flinched as he saw the shiny steel blade come flying across the room. Before he knew what was happening, he felt himself being cloaked by something soft and leathery. Everything around him grew dark again. He heard the sound of the double doors of the attic room slam shut and the hard-hitting sound of the knife hitting wood. He couldn't see anything but could feel himself being rushed down the stairs. Then there was the crash of shattering glass and a fierce wind beneath him. Within minutes he was being set on the ground somewhere far away from the vampire house. Luca and Harper were standing next to him. Jace looked over at Luca almost in admiration.

"You have wings," Jace found it hard to hide his astonishment.

"One of the perks of the demon," Luca said. He smiled at the two of them standing in awe of him. This wasn't Harper's first experience of being flown away by him, but the last time he was kidnapping her, this time he was saving her life.

"The demon?" Harper asked.

"I'll explain later," Luca replied. "For now, we need to get out of here."

Jace followed Luca with Harper walking by his side, though he struggled to keep up with their vampire stride. Luca led them towards a brick building, where they entered the side alleyway through an iron gate. They followed through a side door and down a damp cement stairway to a dark underground tunnel. Jace could feel the hanging lead pipes on the low ceiling grazing the top of his head. He searched his pockets for his phone, so he could use its light to see but then he remembered Quentin had taken it from him. Harper must have noticed him struggling to see in the dark because she reached out, grabbed his hand, and led him the rest of the way. They came to another door, and Luca let them inside. It was pitch black inside, but then Luca reached up, pulling a string to turn on a small light bulb that hung overhead. The room was slightly furnished with two plush chairs and a small round table. Old, tattered boxes were stacked up in the corner. And along the wall was a coffin.

"Is this where you stay?" Jace asked.

"Temporarily," Luca told them. "You'll be safe here. Don't worry. Make yourself comfortable. You'll need to stay here. Harper and I will go out and get some food and supplies for you."

Luca stepped back out into the tunnel, and Harper followed behind him. "We'll be back soon," She whispered as she closed and locked the door behind her leaving Jace there alone, realizing once again he was the prisoner of yet another vampire.

HE RAISED THE DAGGER in his hand above his shoulder and flung it towards the door. The light of the lamp flickered off the steel blade as it soared across the room. Luca expanded his demon wings, swiftly grabbing Harper and Jace and stealing them out of the room. The double doors of the attic room slammed shut. The dagger pierced the wood sticking itself into the door. Dac grunted in frustration. He raced across the room, snatching the dagger out of the door, he peered out into the hallway, but Luca, Harper, and Jace were already gone.

Angrily, he stomped down the stairs all the way to the lower floor, where they kept their rooms. Quentin followed closely behind him. He stopped at Emmaline's room first. When she didn't answer his knock, he opened the door peeking into her empty room. He turned around, almost bumping into Quentin, who was still on his heels. He pushed past Quentin and marched towards Nikolai's room next. There he found Emmaline and, to his surprise, an awakened Nikolai sitting up on his bed.

It had been at least a day since he had last checked on his friend. He and Quentin had been busy trying to decide what to do with Jace, not to mention his own personal matters he was dealing with also. Emmaline and Harper had been taking turns caring for Nikolai the last couple of days, yet neither of them had bothered to inform him that Nikolai had woken up. The anger rose up in him like heat from a furnace. Dac did his best to fix his face so Nikolai wouldn't see his frustration. He may be awake, but he was far from healed.

"Nikolai, when did you wake up? How are you feeling?" Dac asked his friend. He did his best to keep his tone as neutral as possible. He didn't want Nikolai suspecting anything was amiss. He wanted his friend to focus on healing, not on the drama surrounding them.

"Last night," Nikolai answered hoarsely. "Still weak, but I'll be fine. Getting stronger by the minute," he gave Dac a friendly wink. "But what's wrong?" he then asked.

"Nothing," Dac answered. Damn, he obviously didn't do that well a job of hiding his current frustrations. He then turned to Emmaline. "Can we speak to you in the hall for a moment?"

Emmaline nodded and rose up from her chair. She joined Dac and Quentin in the hallway, closing the door to Nikolai's room softly behind her. She looked up at Dac with a puzzled expression.

"What's going on?" She asked.

"Jace has escaped. It appears he is working with my brother Luca. Harper is with them." Dac said.

"He kidnapped Harper again?" Emmaline raised a hand to her mouth.

"No, she brought him here and left with him willingly this time. I don't suspect she will, but if she returns to the house, find me right away." Dac instructed Emmaline.

"Yes. Ok." The shock was written all over Emmaline's face. She didn't bother to hide it, nor did she ask any other questions. She just turned to go back inside Nikolai's room, but Dac grabbed her arm before she could open the door. She turned back around to face him.

"Don't say anything to Nikolai. If he asks about Harper, just tell him you don't know where she is," he said.

Emmaline nodded in agreement and disappeared back through the door to sit with Nikolai. Dac hoped she would be able to hide what she'd learned from him. He didn't want Nikolai worrying while he was still recovering. But Emmaline was the most innocent of the bunch. The years she spent as a vampire had somehow never changed that about her. Because of this, he trusted Emmaline the most. She had always been loyal, and she wasn't selfish like Harper. She would do what was best for everyone. She understood what was at stake. Now he and Quentin had to decide what to do next. He also hoped to hear back from Charlotte and Garrett soon about the music box. Hopefully, they were able to acquire it from Sophia's parents. He needed that box.

Fifteen

Jace awakened on a pile of blankets on the floor. He opened his eyes, his half-conscious mind trying to determine where he was. Then he remembered the attic room, Dac threatening him, and Harper and Luca showing up and dragging him through the tunnel to this room. He must have fallen asleep sometime after the adrenaline wore off, sometime before Harper and Luca returned. A plastic bag filled with canned fruit and veggies, cookies, chips, and other snacks sat on the floor. They had mentioned grabbing some supplies when they were out the night before. His stomach rumbled, and his mouth watered, but he couldn't bring himself to eat just yet.

The light overhead was still on. With no windows, he couldn't tell if it were morning or night. But as he looked around the room, he determined it must at the very least be daylight. On another pile of blankets, Harper lay on her back across the floor. Her hands folded across her chest, she looked almost angelic had it not been for her bloodstained mouth. Jace had to hold back the urge to vomit as he realized what she must have done. Inside the open coffin, Luca slept just as peacefully. He pictured the two of them walking into the late-night convenience store, their shirts and mouths stained with blood. Was the store clerk their victim? Had they gathered up the food for Jace and then claimed the poor man or woman as their meal? He swallowed the tiny amount of spit in his mouth, trying to force the bile in his throat to stay down.

He needed to do something, so he started rummaging one by one through the boxes in the corner. Mostly they were full of old clothing, kitchenware, and books. This must have been a storage room at some point, he thought. Behind one of the boxes was an old wooden picture frame. When Jace picked it up, one of the sides of the frame fell to the floor. He picked it up, staring at its pointed edge. He stared down at the two sleeping vampires. In his mind, he could hear Brigid's voice, *pierce their heart while they sleep, and sever the head from the spine. It's the only way to truly destroy the vampire.*

He dropped the wooden stick to the floor and continued searching the boxes. He wasn't too sure what he was searching for until he found the flashlight. A smile grew across his face as he switched it on, and it lit up. If he were going to escape out of this place, now was his chance.

As quietly as he could, Jace stepped out of the room. Without a key, he had no way of locking it, but he did his best to shut the door as securely as possible. Armed with his flashlight, he made his way through the long corridor of the tunnel. Above his head were the sounds of footsteps and running water. He remembered the brick building from the night before but assumed it had been empty. He stopped, turning his flashlight back in the direction of the room he had just left. Where Harper and Luca still lay in their vampire sleep. No, he couldn't turn back now. He had to trust they would be ok, but he himself had thought of killing them only moments ago. He hesitated a moment longer, then continued searching for a way out of the tunnel.

Finally, he saw the door in the near distance. A few more steps, and he would be outside. He picked up his pace, reaching out for the door handle as he approached the door. He grabbed the doorknob, pushing it forward and yanking it back when it didn't open. He stayed struggling with the door, and his heart dropped to his stomach as he realized it was locked. The flashlight had fallen to the ground and rolled away. He could see the tiny strip of light under the crack of the door teasing him of a freedom that was just out of reach. He sunk to the ground.

With his head pressed against the cold door, he could vaguely make out noises coming from the other side. He began pounding heavily on the door in hopes that someone would hear him. A moment later, the door swung open, and Jace stumbled, almost crashing into the man holding the door open. He sprung out into the welcoming daylight running to get as far away from there as fast as he could. The man called out to him, "Hey! What were you doing...?" But Jace kept his pace, never looking back.

The warm sun was starting to wear him down. His mouth was dry, and his body fatigued. He spotted a small convenience store on the corner. He felt in his pockets for his wallet. Good, it was still there. At least the vampires hadn't taken that from him. He went inside the store and quickly purchased a bottle of water. Once back outside, he chugged down half the water, the other half spilling down his shirt. He tightened the cap back on the bottle and hailed a cab. It was time to get out of this city and back to Aura Springs.

Jace had the cab drop him off in front of his house. He paid the driver and trudged across his lawn to the front door, his body weary from his ordeal. The cab ride back to Aura Springs had cost him nearly a hundred dollars, but he didn't care. He was only glad to be home. Unfortunately, he knew he couldn't stay there for long. He would need to be gone by nightfall. As soon as Harper and Luca woke up, they would come searching for him. Not to mention Dac and Quentin were probably looking for him too.

Once inside, he made his way directly to the bathroom. He dropped his sweat and dirt-stained clothes on the floor and turned on the shower faucet. He leaned his shoulder against the tiled wall letting the shower water rain down on him. He needed to think of a plan since he hadn't thought much past his escape. He knew he wasn't safe here, and he knew he hadn't much time, so he pulled himself together and washed up.

After his shower and some much-needed coffee, he decided he needed to get in touch with Sarah. The problem was he had no phone, nor did he remember her phone number. Who remembers phone numbers anymore? Also, he had no car to even get to her. His car was still where he parked it a few nights ago when he met with Una. At least he hoped it was still there. But his laptop was sitting on the kitchen table next to him. He opened it up and searched for her shop. He jotted down the phone number from the contact information on her website and went next door to his neighbor's house to ask to borrow their phone.

SARAH PULLED HER CAR up to the curb outside of Jace's house. He hopped in, duffel bag in hand. She gave him a sideways glance, and he knew she was waiting for an explanation. He had been rather vague with her on the phone as to why he no longer had his phone or his car.

"So..." she said after clearing her throat.

"Well, short version is I tried to meet Alex. It turned out to be Una I was meeting. Quentin followed me and brought me back to the vampire house. He and Dac kept me prisoner there and then tried to kill me, but not before Harper came in with Dac's brother Luca, who, by the way, has wings and can fly. Luca grabbed Harper and me bringing us to some room underneath some building on the opposite side of Aura City, essentially saving my ass. Then while they were asleep this morning, I escaped, caught a cab, and came home."

"Ok. And now the long version," Sarah demanded.

"I'll tell you on the way. Let's just go."

Sarah drove while Jace filled her in on his latest vampire adventure. They stopped by a store to get Jace a new phone. They drove past his car. It was still parked where he had last left it. They decided, however, it would probably be best to leave it there. Any of the vampires would be able to find him if he were driving it around, especially at night. Maybe they could detract them if they left it parked.

A short time later, they arrived at Sarah's house. Brigid was waiting for them on the back porch. She had placed hawthorn throughout the lattice and was burning an incense. She sat in one of the wicker chairs with her cane resting at her side and her dark shades over her eyes.

Jace and Sarah each took a seat on the other patio chairs. After a few minutes of awkward silence, Jace retold his story so that Brigid could hear it. This definitely changed things as far as Brigid was concerned. This was more than just finding and destroying Cloe's killer. These vampires were becoming more dangerous. They would need to eradicate them all.

"It's time you realize, my dear boy, they are no longer your allies, and they were never your friends," Brigid said. "The sooner you come to accept that, the better off you'll be."

Jace hung his head, not responding. He knew in his heart Brigid was right. If he were going to survive this, he would need to kill the vampires before they killed him.

"Now, obviously, the dagger will now be impossible to get until we destroy Dac and the other four that live with him," Brigid continued. "But there is another way, and it starts with retrieving a certain music box."

Sixteen

Harper opened her eyes and sat up from where she lay on the floor. She looked around the room where she had just spent the night. Luca was already up, sitting crossed-legged in one of the only two chairs in the room. His expression was blank, which somehow made Harper more nervous than if he had shown any type of emotion. The one thing she learned about Luca was that, unlike Dac, he always kept himself composed. Harper looked around the room more closely, and that's when she realized Jace was gone.

"Where is Jace?" She asked Luca.

"Don't know. It appears he left sometime during the day."

"You think he'll come back?"

"Doubt it, but at least he didn't try to kill us in our sleep."

"Why would you say that?" Harper asked, confused by his comment.

Luca didn't answer. He just held up the sharpened piece of wood from the broken picture frame.

"Where did that come from?"

"My guess would be from over there in that corner somewhere," He said, pointing to a pile of boxes in the corner.

"Well, no matter, Jace wouldn't try to hurt us."

"I know you want to believe that, but it doesn't matter how many times either of you deny it. It doesn't change that fact that your old friend is a vampire hunter."

"No, I know him. He wouldn't hurt anyone," Harper protested.

"Maybe that was true once, but his fiancée was killed by a vampire, and he's seeking out said vampire for his revenge. That makes him a vampire hunter," Luca pointed out. "Plus, he's hanging around other vampire hunters now, and after last night, well, it's only a matter of time he perceives us all to be a threat."

"I need to fix this," Harper said softly, looking down at her hands and picking at her fingernails.

"What's done is done. You got bigger problems than Jace at the moment."

"Dac?"

"Exactly. I think it might be best to get you away from here for a while."

"But this is my home."

"Not anymore. You went against Dac's wishes, and you turned to me to help you do that. To Dac, that was a betrayal and more than likely an unforgivable one.

"Well, I'm not going anywhere. I'm not afraid of Dac."

"You should be. But, if you're going to insist on sticking around, I suggest you stay with me and don't try to go back to that house. Now, let's go. We've got lots to do."

Luca led her back through the tunnel, but instead of leaving out of the same door they entered through last night, he led her up a stairway leading up to the building lobby. Harper had just assumed the building was empty like a lot of the other buildings in the city, but this one was full of warm-blooded humans. She watched Luca traverse across the lobby with ease and confidence. She followed closely behind him, admiring the lavishness of the building. The marble floor reflected the clear and yellow lights of the chandeliers that hung from the ceiling. Plush leather chairs and a sofa created an inviting sitting area. The doorman sat perched at his desk, greeting residents as they stepped in through the double glass doors from outside.

Luca nodded to the doorman as they passed by on their way to the elevator. Harper set her gaze to the floor. In the elevator, Luca pushed the button for the 13th floor. They remained silent until they finally reached their destination. Luca unlocked the door to one of the apartments and led Harper inside. She looked around in awe at the dark hardwood flooring and custom countertops. The minimalistic furnishings left a cozy yet luxurious feel. The expansive windows gave an enticing view of the city below but also explained why he slept downstairs. There was no place in here to hide from the daytime sun.

"I had some fresh clothes brought up for you," Luca said, pointing to the front closet.

"But how...?" Harper started to ask, but Luca waved her off. She opened the closet to a full wardrobe of tops, pants, and dresses. She pulled out a silk tank top and pair of black jeans she thought would go with the sandals she wore on her feet. Luca pointed her in the direction of the bathroom, where she could freshen up and change. Then he disappeared into the other room, where she assumed he would do the same.

When Harper emerged from the bathroom, Luca was standing at the window. His back was turned as he was gazing out into the night sky. Harper stepped towards him. The lights of the neighboring buildings reflected off the glass.

"It's a beautiful view," Harper said.

"You should see it from the rooftop." Luca turned to face her.

"Are we going to fly up there?"

"No," he chuckled. "We will take the elevator." His pearly fangs sparkled when he smiled at her. He took her hand and guided her out of the apartment and back towards the elevators.

They stepped out onto the roof into the warm night air. The sapphire sky was clear. The city lights twinkled like a sea of stars. Harper stood at the edge, looking out at the world around her. Luca placed a hand on her shoulder. She looked up at him.

"I thought you said we had lots to do tonight?" She asked him.

"We do. And one of those things is teaching you to hunt like a proper vampire." Luca led her back through the building and out into the bustling city street.

They walked into a restaurant and followed the hostess to a small table in the corner. The dark ambiance masked their extraordinarily pale skin. Harper paid close attention to the way Luca charmed his way into conversation with the guests seated next to them, eventually inviting them over, which of course, the couple graciously accepted.

Luca continued to refill the couple's wine glasses before they could finish, neither of them realizing that Harper nor Luca took a single sip from their own glasses, nor did they eat a bite of food from their plates. But Harper realized the two were more than simply drunk from the wine they consumed. They were mesmerized by Luca, and she wondered how she herself could accomplish such a trick. She would have to ask him once they were alone again. For now, she was getting impatient, waiting for the moment she could sink her teeth into one of these unsuspecting victims.

Luca must have sensed her eagerness because he motioned for the waitress to bring over the check and politely asked the couple at their table if they would like to continue with the evening elsewhere. Luca then paid the bill and escorted the group out of the restaurant. Effortlessly Luca separated the pair leaving Harper alone with her prey.

For the first time, Harper didn't feel the guilt that came along with the kill. Standing in the dark alley between the restaurant and the building next to it, Harper leaned her back against the brick wall. The man in front of her stood so close she could hear his heart beating. He leaned over her pressing the palms of his hands against the same wall just above her shoulders, limiting the space between them. Had she been human, this would have been a threatening position. But she wasn't human, and this man had more to fear from her than she had of him. She smiled at him, temporarily concealing the large fangs in her mouth. He leaned his face closer to hers. She placed her hand gently behind his neck. Her lips grazed his throat as he let her take the lead as if he had a choice. Her fangs punctured his artery, and the blood from within seeped into her mouth with the sweet taste of wine. The man let out a moan. The moment felt like an ethereal experience as he willingly gave himself over to her.

A sound rang in her ears, a melody reminiscent of childhood, the song of a music box. Harper dropped the body of her victim and stepped out of the alleyway into the sparsely crowded street. She began walking in a daze in search of the source of the music. Suddenly a hand grabbed her from behind, breaking her from her trance.

"Come on. We have to get away from here." Luca said as he pulled her in the opposite direction.

"But that music, I feel like I need to find it. What is it?" Harper asked, trying to pull away from the tight grip Luca held to her arm.

"Your demise if you do find it. Now let's go." Luca said.

They moved swiftly through the streets until they reached the tunnel they had entered through the night before. Luca kept a firm grip on Harper's arm until they were safely locked behind the closed door of the room where they slept during the daylight hours.

"We'll be safe here. At least for now." Luca paced the room while Harper sat in one of the chairs. Her eyes never wavering from his constant back and forth movements.

"I don't understand. What's going on?" She could feel every nerve in her body start to prickle. Luca's distress over the music scared her.

"The last time I heard that music box, it was in the possession of a little girl in Noxwood. Somehow, I fear she doesn't have it anymore. And whoever does, knows of its power."

"Power?"

"The power to transfix you and lead you directly to your killer."

Seventeen

D ac sat in his office chair, hearing the words spoken by his two associates, though not listening, as his mind tried to process what he was being told. Each word sounded as though it were being spoken a million miles away. How was the music box gone? And who had it? Charlotte and Garrett sat across from him, explaining how they went to the address in Noxwood and requested to purchase the music box. Unfortunately, by the time they arrived, the music box was already gone. According to the woman they spoke with, the young girl had informed her earlier that day that her music box was lost. They had searched the entire house but could find it nowhere; therefore, even if she would have considered selling the box, it was not available for purchase.

"I'm sorry we couldn't get you that music box, but I left the woman my number in case it shows up, and she decides to sell it," Charlotte was saying, but Dac waved her off.

"It's fine. You two can go. Let me know if she calls, though I doubt she ever will."

Dac exited his office and escorted both Charlotte and Garrett from the house, and then went straight to Nikolai's room. He didn't want to worry him, but keeping secrets had almost cost him his friend's life the last time.

The door to Nikolai's room was closed as usual. Dac knocked lightly on the door as he entered. Nikolai was alone, sitting up with a book in hand and no longer attached to the IV. He appeared to be recovering at a much quicker pace since waking up from his coma.

Nikolai looked up from his book. The expression in his eyes was that of contempt in contrast to his friendly greeting the other night. His right eyebrow was slightly raised as if daring Dac to speak. Dac knew the day would come when he would have to face what he had done all those years ago. He sat in the chair across from Nikolai. Gripping the arms of the chair, he pulled in a deep breath before slowly exhaling.

"I need to speak with you."

"You knew, didn't you? You knew my son was alive?" Nikolai now held the book to his lap, but he kept a firm grip as though suppressing the urge to do something else with his hands.

"No."

"And Una?"

"No."

"But you were there that night, not just at the end, but you were there the whole time?"

"Yes, I was," Confession time. Dac averted his gaze, peering down at the floor and away from Nikolai. "I am the reason you couldn't save them. But please try to understand...."

"Then there is nothing left to say. You may leave my room now, and once I am strong enough, I will be leaving here." Nikolai turned his head and lifted the book back up to cover his face.

"And go where exactly? To your wife and son? They still want you dead. I may have been wrong that night, but I am the reason you are alive today." Dac leaned forward in his chair.

"As I've said, there's nothing left to say. Whether I live or die is no longer your concern. Now please leave."

"Nikolai, the music box is here." Dac ignored Nikolai's demands. The news of the music was more important than his friend's animosity towards him.

"The music box, here? How do you know that?" Nikolai lowered the book once more and glanced sideways at Dac.

"I heard it while still back in Noxwood. Remember the little girl, Sophia?"

"Yes."

"She had it. I followed the sound and found myself outside her window. I resisted it then. When I came back here, I asked Garrett and Charlotte to go to Noxwood and convince the girl's parents to sell the music box to them. Unfortunately, by the time they got there, the music box was gone."

"Gone? Who has it now?" The concern was evident in Nikolai's tone.

"I don't know. But my guess would be Alex or Jace."

"Jace? Why would Jace have it, and how would he even know about it?" Nikolai raised an eyebrow at the accusation that Jace could have the music box.

"So much has happened since that night in Noxwood," Dac explained the death of Jace's fiancée, Jace's meeting with Una, and his involvement with the vampire hunters. Nikolai listened intently, but Dac knew it was only because he understood the dangers now imposed upon them. That music box had almost killed them both nearly 70 years ago before they had settled in Aura City. They had managed to get away, blinding the hunter in the process, and until now, had never heard the music box again.

"Where is Jace now? Which room is he in? I want to speak to him." Nikolai began to stand up, but Dac put a hand on his knee to stop him.

"He's gone."

"Gone?"

Dac pulled his hand back from Nikolai's knee and folded his hands in his lap. He looked over at his friend, then averted his gaze to the floor. He then continued informing Nikolai of all that transpired in the attic, how Luca showed up dragging Jace away.

"There's one more thing," Dac continued. "Harper is with them. And this time, she went voluntarily."

This time Nikolai did stand, and Dac didn't stop him. He watched as Nikolai left the room and followed closely behind. Nikolai marched down the hall to Harper's room, confirming Dac's story that she was gone. As he noticed the dark bloodstains, he knelt down, swiping his index finger across the floor. He looked up at Dac, who was watching from the doorway. Neither of them said a word as Nikolai continued looking through Harper's room. Dac, unsure of what it could be that Nikolai was searching for but sensing his friend's grief and guilt, decided to give him some privacy. He shut the door and returned to his office, where he would call Quentin and Emmaline to meet him. He informed them of the music box and the dangers it brought to the group. Moments later, Nikolai appeared in the doorway. He entered the room, and the four vampires began to come up with a plan.

JACE SAT ON THE BACK porch of Sarah's house. Sarah sat across from him, though Brigid had long gone to bed. The warm summer breeze made the flames of the citronella candles flicker. The green glow of lightning bugs twinkled throughout the darkened backyard. A mosquito buzzed past Jace's ear, and he swatted it away. There was an eerie calmness around them as if waiting for the storm, which wasn't surprising considering they were hunting vampires, and vampires were hunting them.

Jace sat thinking about the music box. Brigid explained how it could be instrumental in bringing the vampires to them if they could not get to them during the daylight hours. The music box would entrance the vampire, allowing them to destroy it. Although it still carried with it some degree of danger. A stronger vampire could resist its magic. However, a lesser one could not. The same would go for killing the vampire in the day. If they were to happen upon the vampire while he slept, they could almost easily destroy it without consequence. However, a stronger vampire could wake and, even in his weakened state, would still be more powerful than a human. Either option was risky, considering the vampires they were currently up against. Not only were they old and strong, but one of them was powered by a demon.

Brigid believed it was one of these vampires that had killed his fiancée Cloe. Jace found it hard to believe that it would have been Harper or her friends, though it could have been someone from Luca's crew or even Luca himself. But why would Luca have offered to help him if he were the one who had killed her? Although it wasn't likely, Luca would be helping him now, and maybe he never intended to help him in the first place. It was possible Luca had no intention of holding up his end of the bargain, though Jace had a feeling Luca wasn't the type to go back on his word. Otherwise, would he not have just killed Alex himself?

Jace's thoughts went back to the music box, and he wondered what Sarah was thinking. Earlier, when Brigid told them about it, she said she knew where it was being kept. When she called the woman, who had been entrusted with it, Brigid was informed the box was missing. And not only was it missing, but someone had come by earlier that morning asking to purchase it.

The breeze, which had been steady all night, began to calm. The typical noises of the night began to quiet. Jace and Sarah both sat up straighter in their chairs. Neither said a word as they listened for movement of any kind. Jace turned his head from side to side, trying to get a glimpse of anything in the dark. It was then that a dark figure appeared at the edge of the porch steps, a figure he remembered as the apparition that appeared to him on the night that he summoned Alex.

"I believe I have something you are looking for; the question is, what are you willing to do for me in return?" The shadowy figure spoke.

Jace pondered this for a moment. This was precisely what Luca had wanted him to do, enter into a pact with Alex under the guise that they would work together while he eventually fed Luca information on the elusive vampire's whereabouts. Maybe this could get him back in Luca's good graces after having left so abruptly when Luca had, in all actuality, saved his life. Jace was sure Luca would see it as a betrayal. Maybe if he pretended to work with Alex as was the original deal and then was able to tell Luca where Alex was, he could buy himself some time. But the last thing Jace wanted to do was make a deal with another vampire.

"That depends on what you're offering." Jace eventually said.

"It's simple, really. I hand you the one who killed your girlfriend, and you hand me, my father." Alex answered.

"How exactly is that simple?"

"With this." Alex held out the music box. Jace reached for the box, but Alex snatched it away. "Not yet. I see you still need time to think it over. Talk it over with your partners. I'll come back tomorrow night for your answer.

Alex faded away back into the darkness. Jace looked over to Sarah. Her mouth was slightly gaped open. Her eyes bulged, and her complexion had paled. Jace realized at that moment this was the first time Sarah had ever come face to face with any vampire. When he put his arm around her shoulder, he could feel her trembling. She looked up at him, and her face blushed as she flashed a tiny smile.

"I'll do better next time. I promise." Sarah said.

"It's ok." Jace lightly squeezed Sarah's shoulder. "I remember the first time I'd met a vampire."

"It's one thing knowing that they exist, but face to face like that...."

"I know. It's almost surreal."

They sat out there for a few minutes longer before deciding it was time to get some sleep. The next day they would talk to Brigid about Alex's visit and decide together what would be the best thing to do. Jace still wasn't sure about getting involved with another vampire. He was hoping Brigid would have another way to do what they needed to do. He realized he was getting anxious. He just wanted to rid his life of all these vampires and go back to something somewhat normal.

Jace snuffed out the candles, then followed Sarah into the house. To both of their surprise, Brigid was awake, standing in the kitchen. The lights in the room were still out, and they almost hadn't seen her. She was standing there with a glass of water in one hand, her cane in the other.

"You should make the deal," Brigid said when she heard the two of them enter the house. "Make the deal and then contact Luca, sticking to your original plan with him. Let them take each other out. Once you get the music box and find out who killed your fiancée, you can have your justice if that is what you truly wish."

Eighteen

Harper sat in the tiny storage room, staring at Luca pace the floor. They hadn't left the room in days except to hunt. She wanted to be back out in the world. She wanted to watch the city from the rooftop. As much as she understood Luca was protecting her, she longed to go back to her friends, to the vampires who had become her family. But she knew she couldn't do that now. Not after helping Jace escape. Dac wouldn't forgive her for her betrayal, but she couldn't let Jace die.

When she thought more about it, being with Luca wasn't all that bad. With him, she didn't have to be ashamed of her vampiric instincts. Drinking blood was for survival, but feeding off the living for her was living. It was the one thing Dac had never allowed her to experience, and once she had, she had to hide it from everyone. But now, with Luca, there was no more hiding. He taught her how to enjoy the hunt and savor the moment of the drink. She felt comfortable and confident with Luca. Most importantly, she no longer felt the need to cut herself. With the guilt gone, it no longer needed a release. She was free.

Only she was stuck hiding in this room from a music box. Luca was still determined to save his brother whether he thought he needed saving or not. And in spite of Dac's new contempt for her, she was determined to help. She had loved Dac once. Perhaps she still did in some way.

Luca turned to her with flashing eyes. "Let's go," he said.

"Where are we going?"

"To see my brother."

Harper cocked her head. Why would he suddenly want to go to Dac after being so adamant she stayed far away from him? In fact, it was only days ago that he suggested she go to his house in Noxwood and hide out. Now he wanted both of them to go and see Dac. He must have a plan, she guessed.

Luca must have sensed her hesitation because he grabbed hold of her hand as he reached for the door. Just as the door flew open, they both took a step back. There, on the other side, was Jace standing in the dark corridor. Luca let out a growl at the sight of him. Harper squeezed Luca's hand in an attempt to calm him.

"Jace, what are you doing here?" Harper asked.

Trying to maintain eye contact, Jace responded. "I saw Alex."

Harper grabbed Jace's arm and pulled him into the room. Luca slammed the door shut. He looked at Jace with both intrigue and suspicion.

"Why did you leave here?" Luca growled. Harper placed her hand on his arm in a second attempt to keep him calm.

"Well, if I hadn't, I wouldn't have spoken to Alex now, would I? That is what you wanted, wasn't it, to know where Alex is hiding?" Jace's words came out of his mouth with a tone of sarcasm. Harper hoped she'd be able to stop Luca from killing him if it had come to that.

"And do you know where he is? Or are you working with him now and leading him straight to us.?" Luca barked at Jace. Harper winced but kept her firm grip on Luca's arm.

"Luca, please stop." Harper pleaded with the older vampire. "Jace, what did Alex want?"

"He wanted to make a deal with me. Just as you had suggested," Jace said, looking toward Luca. This time he managed to keep a neutral tone. "He promised to give me the name of the vampire who killed Cloe if I deliver Nikolai to him."

Harper gasped. She felt her normally cold body flash hot. "How does he expect you to accomplish that?" She asked him.

"With a music box."

Now it was Luca's turn to gasp. "And did he give it to you?"

"Yes, I have it. And it's being kept in a safe place." Jace explained further how Alex showed up at Sarah's house and proposed his deal to them. He further explained that since Alex knew he was staying with Sarah, he would need to continue to stay there and work with her if his plan was going to work. Other than that, he had decided to go ahead with the original plan he and Luca had agreed upon.

"What I don't understand is, if he had the music box, why not just use it himself? Why the need to recruit Jace?" Harper asked.

"He must have something bigger planned," Luca answered before he turned to Jace. "You should get out of here, go back to Sarah's, but remember that Dac is still looking for you, so stay aware and be careful. I'll honor our original deal. In the meantime, I suggest you do whatever Alex asks. Don't come back here. I'll come to you in a few days."

Harper followed Jace back out into the corridor. "You need to be prepared for whatever is ahead. Do what the hunters say. Learn as much as you can in the upcoming days. Most importantly, please remember in the end, we are all vampires, and you are human. Do what you must to survive. I love you." She went back into the small room she shared with Luca before Jace could say anything to her. A single tear fell from her right eye. She quickly swiped it away before Luca could notice. But he came up to where she stood and wrapped his arms around her in a tight embrace. She buried her head in his chest, and she let the tears fall.

It had been a long time since Harper had allowed herself to break down like that. She pulled away from Luca. As she turned her back to him, she brushed the hair away from her face with her hands and wiped the tears from her eyes. She paced awkwardly around the small room, not knowing what to say. This tiny space was starting to get to her. She needed some air. She reached for the door and stepped out into the tunnel leading to the outside world. She could hear Luca's footsteps behind her as she raced through the tunnel. She was surprised he didn't stop her but also relieved.

When she reached the outside and stepped out onto the sidewalk, Luca stood next to her. He placed a hand on her shoulder, but she nudged him away. She turned and looked up at him; his normal dark hardened eyes stared softly into hers.

"There's something I need to do," she said to him. "Alone."

"I know." A hint of a smile formed on his lips. The large black bat-like wings extended from his back. He gracefully ascended into the sky and perched upon the rooftop, and Harper knew he would be watching over her.

Harper found herself creeping around the outside of the very house she had called her home for the past few years. The front windows were dark as usual. She lurked around to the back side of the house, where she could see a light through the kitchen window. Careful not to be caught, she peered into the window to see Emmaline seated alone at the island. Harper tapped softly on the window attracting Emmaline's attention. When Emmaline opened the door to inspect the noise, Harper grabbed her by the arm, pulling her against the side of the house. She covered Emmaline's mouth with her hand before the other vampire could scream or call out to the others.

"I need your help, Emmaline. Please." Harper pleaded with Emmaline to allow her into the house, to help her get around undetected. Emmaline was reluctant, but she agreed only because the others were not home.

"Be quick. I can't help you if Dac comes home and finds you here." Emmaline told her.

"I will. I understand, and thank you."

Harper moved through the house as quickly as she could. She first went down the hidden stairs to the lower level, where they all kept their rooms. She opened the door to her old room. Looking around, her eyes became moist with tears as memories came flooding back. The first night she had awoken in this very room as a vampire, Nikolai had come to explain what had happened to her. She was so hostile to him, but he was patient with her. They had become close throughout the following months, feeling a tight bond with each other.

Her relationship with Dac had been unexpected. When they had first met, he was polite but distant. They hadn't spoken much in those first few months she lived with them, though Harper always felt the attraction between them. After a while, he began to soften, and he had later admitted the reason he kept his distance from her. He had confessed his feelings to her, and she acknowledged hers in return. He had kissed her that night. Over the next two years, the affair between them grew, as did their feelings for each other. Harper's heart fluttered thinking about it. So much had changed since then.

Harper grabbed the bag she had been looking for and left for Dac's room. She opened the door to his room. She had rarely been inside this room, as he normally came to her. The room was set up similar to all the others on this floor, dark and windowless with antique furniture. His room didn't have a chandelier like hers. He kept only a small tiffany lamp on the bedside table. The lamp gave off a limited amount of light through its stained-glass shade. Dac seemed to prefer the dark. She often questioned how he could be both modern and so old-fashioned at the same time. It was as if, as much as he grew and adjusted to the changes of the years, he tried his best to stay as connected to his past as he could. He would tell her it was just as crucial to the existence of the vampire as was blood.

As she searched his room for the object she was looking for, it was becoming more apparent to her that it was not there. She decided the next best place to search would be his office. She just hoped he didn't have it with him.

She made her way up the two flights of stairs to Dac's office as quickly as she could. She wasn't sure how long she had until the others came home, and she knew Emmaline must be getting impatient. Also, she didn't want Emmaline getting in any trouble for allowing her inside, so she knew she had to hurry.

She searched the desk drawers with no luck. She checked inside the drawers of the two side tables that stood on either side of the wall. Then she noticed the dark wood box on the bookshelf behind the desk. It was the same color wood as the shelf so that she almost didn't see it, and probably the reason she had never noticed it before tonight. If you weren't looking for it, you weren't likely to see it.

Harper picked up the antique box. It was heavy in her hands. The object inside rattled as she turned the box on its side. She inspected the old-fashioned lock and then remembered a key she saw inside the top desk drawer. She opened the drawer in search of the key. Once she found it, she set the box on top of the desk and fit the key into the lock. She gently opened the lid, and there it was, exactly what she had been searching for when she came to the house. She put the object in her bag and swiftly left the room, going back down the stairs and out of the house through the kitchen door.

She quickly found her way to the nearest train station and got on the first train heading to Aura Springs. She was relieved to see the train relatively empty. Only a few people occupied a few seats at the other end of the train car. Harper took a seat nearest the doors, keeping her head down until she reached her destination.

A cab was parked next to the curb outside the station at Aura Springs. The driver yelled out to Harper, asking if she needed a ride. The last time she had refused, but this time she hopped in the back seat of the car and gave the driver the address to Sarah's house.

Harper paid the driver and stepped out of the cab. Quietly she walked up to the house where Jace told her he would be staying. The house seemed dark, but she could hear voices coming from the inside. She knocked lightly on the front door. Sarah answered the door with Jace standing behind her. When he noticed Harper, he stepped in front of Sarah, putting himself between the two women.

"What are you doing here? I don't have any information for you yet." Jace shut the door behind him as he stepped outside.

"I have something for you. Take this. You'll need it to protect yourself."

Jace looked at Harper puzzlingly as she handed him the bag. He took it from her and reached inside. Jace looked at her wide-eyed as he pulled his hand out of the bag holding the dagger. Before he could ask her any other questions, Harper was gone.

Nineteen

The music played in his head over and over since the first time he heard it back in Noxwood. He should have handled things differently, instead of going to Luca and accusing him, he should have tried to acquire the music box himself. Instead, he believed it was his brother trying to get in his head, but now he understood it wasn't. At the time, he did not consider the young girl Sophia really had the actual music box when in fact, she did. And now someone else had it, someone much more dangerous than some little girl.

For nearly 200 years after Dac and Nikolai thought they had destroyed Luca, the two of them had traveled together, never staying in the same place longer than a year or two. Dac was always looking over his shoulder, knowing one day his brother may come back but hoping he'd stay in his coffinless grave for eternity.

Along the way, they had occasionally met other vampires who had warned them of hunters, but they themselves had never run into one. That was, of course, until they caught the attention of a young woman with a rare knowledge of potions and a very specific music box.

They had arrived on the rocky shores of Crimson Fells. The night air was crisp and the sky cloudy. A light mist coated the atmosphere. As they journeyed through the streets of this new town, they noticed its quiet demeanor. A car or two passed by. Their tires loud as they rolled over the cobblestoned road. Dac and Nikolai stayed to the far end of the sidewalk, careful to keep clear of the yellow streetlamps as they searched for the address that was to be their next temporary home.

The first few months went by uneventfully. They slept during the day within their new compound, and at night they would carefully hunt their prey. Rarely did they mingle amongst the humans of this town, not wanting to draw attention to themselves. But at the same time, they did not want to appear suspicious. So, at times they would go out to the theatre or the local pub. It was a time of war. Death was a constant on people's minds—a vampire's paradise for those who hunted near the battlegrounds. Dac and Nikolai did not stay too long in such areas, however. Rumors of their battles with Luca gained them many friends among other vampires around the world but also many enemies. The killing of one's own kind was looked down upon, and even as the years passed on, some older vampires still regarded them as a threat.

It was a clear, warm summer night when they first happened upon their first and only hunter. After months of enjoying the quaintness of Crimson Fells, they had begun to let their guard down. The humans were preoccupied with their own turmoil. No one gave a glance to the two strangers who had moved into their town. They kept to themselves and caused no trouble. Of course, they rarely fed from humans, and the death of livestock went unquestioned. Wolves were easier to blame than some mythical creature that stalked the night.

This night, however, they knew they were being watched. Dac and Nikolai were on their way out for the night when they noticed a young woman across the street from their residence. She stood as though she were waiting for someone. Under the light of the streetlamp, Dac observed this woman was unusually dressed in pants, and the shoes on her feet were absent of the typical heel in fashion at the time. Her red hair stood out in the dark of night. And once their eyes met, Dac knew she was one he'd been warned about.

At that moment, the woman ran off, and Dac allowed her to get away. He and Nikolai relocated to a new place of residence that very same night, knowing it was no longer safe to stay where they were but too late in the night to travel far. They would make plans the next night to leave for another city, possibly another country. Too bad those plans got interrupted.

The vampires set out the next night to catch the midnight train out of town. As they left the confines of their underground hiding spot, the melody of a song was playing somewhere nearby. The song was entrancing, and they began to follow it. They came to a building. All the windows were dark except for one. They entered. It was like entering into the past. The room was lit by only candlelight, and in the corner, she stood, the vampire hunter. Her copper-colored hair was pinned on top of her head. Her silhouette was draped in darkness as she attempted to remain in the cover of the shadows. Realizing they had walked into a trap, Dac managed to clear his mind of the music and escape its trance. Nikolai rushed towards the woman, obviously recognizing the same, but the woman disappeared. They were alone in the room. Rather than search for her, the vampires decided to leave the house and head back towards the station, hoping to still catch their train. Escaping the hunter would be better than killing her, they thought.

They carried on their journey with keen eyes, carefully surveying their surroundings. Just before reaching the train station Dac heard Nikolai cry out. He turned back to see Nikolai had been doused with a type of liquid. The same they had used years ago on his brother Luca. The smell of frankincense and peppermint was strong. Dac rushed to the aid of his friend, pulling off his jacket and using it to wipe the poison from his skin. A shadow loomed over them. Standing there with a knife in her hand was the vampire hunter. She raised the knife above her head, bringing it back down with all her strength toward the vampire. Dac raised his hand, grabbing the hunter by her wrist. The knife dangled above his chest. Nikolai grabbed it, tossing it to the side. Dac had the woman in a tight grip, his hands firm against the sides of her face. He stared deep into her eyes as she struggled to move. He bared his fangs but hesitated to bite her. She managed to reach one of her hands into the pocket of her trousers. A vial of liquid fell to the ground. Nikolai was still lying on the ground, his skin still burned from the oils. He grabbed the vial. Inside was not the same oils she had doused him with the first time. Nikolai could smell the harsh chemicals through the glass. He loosened the cap of the vial and tossed it in the woman's direction. The vial hit the woman. Its contents splashed across her face. She screamed and tightly shut her eyes. The chemical dripped off her eyelashes. Dac finally dropped her to the ground making the fatal error of leaving her alive. He grabbed Nikolai by the arm and dragged him to the train. They reached the platform just in time to board the train before it left the station. The next night just after sundown, they were on a plane crossing the ocean to a brand-new place.

They landed just before daylight. Knowing this would be a dangerous trip, Dac enlisted the help of another vampire he met in Crimson Fells. He told Dac that he knew someone in a place called Aura city who would help them. As Dac and Nikolai exited the airport, a car was waiting for them. A man in a dark grey suit was awaiting their arrival. He introduced himself as Charlie and said he worked for a man named Quentin.

Charlie quickly ushered Dac and Nikolai into the car and drove them to a townhouse on the outskirts of this large foreign city. There Quentin was waiting to receive them. Being that daylight was mere minutes away, Quentin kept the introductions short and led them directly to an underground room that would keep them safe from the sun. They would soon learn that although Quentin was considered a vampire, he had never been human and therefore didn't have the same adverse reaction to sunlight as they nor did he need blood to keep him alive. Rather he survived on the energy of living beings, and while daylight would not harm him, he also preferred the night.

Quentin provided the two vampires with the shelter and friendship they needed to establish themselves in the city. After several discussions, Dac and Nikolai decided they would stay in Aura City long term. Dac eventually figured out that if they could get the humans to donate blood, they could survive without the risk of being discovered. Dac founded the donation center and found a house he felt suitable for them to live in. It was only after a fire tore through Quentin's townhouse that he came to live with them.

"Have you decided?" Quentin's voice broke Dac's thoughts, bringing him back to the present.

"Yes, we must find where Luca has taken Jace. I believe he will lead us to both the music box and Alex." Dac glanced up at Quentin standing in the kitchen entryway. Dac had been sitting at the kitchen table for what felt like hours. He had a glass filled halfway with the blood they kept for nourishment. He had barely taken a sip, however. Instead, his mind stayed on the music box.

"And then what?" Quentin sat down in one of the other chairs surrounding the table.

"We destroy them both." Dac's hands rested on the table on either side of his glass.

"And what about Nikolai?"

"I will not sacrifice Nikolai's life for that of his son's."

"I agree," Quentin said. "But there has to be some other way."

"There is no other way." Dac pounded his fist against the tabletop. "Alex is a threat and always will be. He detests his father and will not stop coming after Nikolai if we do not stop him."

"So, how do you suppose we find your brother?" Quentin asked, diverting Dac's attention away from Alex.

"Easy follow the trail of bodies."

Dac stood up, pushed past Quentin, and headed for the stairs leading to his office. He sat at his desk, opened his computer, and searched for any news of local killings. Luca had always been arrogant and careless. He read through countless articles knowing he would find what he was looking for eventually. Finally, he found it. The article reported two separate bodies found within a few feet of each other. Each one had appeared to have suffered a significant amount of blood loss and appeared to have been injured by an object, causing puncture wounds to the neck. The incident occurred on the other end of the city. Dac raced to the top of the stairs and called down to Quentin.

"I know where to find them!" he shouted.

He ran back into his office. Before leaving to find his brother, there was something he needed. He walked over to the wooded box on the back bookshelf. He picked it up and placed it on his desk, carefully opening the lid. When he looked inside, he let out a bitter grunt. The box was empty. The dagger was gone. He slammed the lid shut. Papers that rested on the desk fell to the floor. Dac stomped out of the room and up the stairs to the attic to grab another weapon. Quentin followed behind him.

"The dagger is gone," Dac informed Quentin.

"Harper?"

"That would be my guess. She must have come and taken it sometime when we were all out."

"Well, we know where to find her."

"You're right. I'm sure she is still with my brother. Let's go."

Dac and Quentin left out of the house to search for Luca without telling the other two. They didn't want to alert Nikolai to their plan to find Alex. Nikolai had expressed interest in locating the music box, but they both knew if it led them to Alex like they thought it would, he would find a way to protect Alex before they could get to him.

In the area where the bodies had been found, Dac and Quentin searched for any sign of Luca's presence. Of course, they found nothing. Luca, although careless of leaving his victims in plain sight, never left any evidence of himself. As they surveyed the area, Dac took notice of the restaurants, stores, hotels, and residential buildings. This area of the city was bustling, but most of all, it was expensive, and one thing Dac knew about his brother was that he loved luxury.

"What do you think?" Quentin asked him. "Would he stay this close to so many people?

"Live permanently, no. But temporarily, as I assume his stay here is, yes, he would."

"Seems risky to me."

"Luca thrives on risks, and he treats hunting like a sport. He plays games with his victims before feeding from them. He is heartless, and he is turning Harper to be just like him."

Quentin nodded his acknowledgment, and the two of them continued in their search. Dac could feel his brother's presence nearby as the temperature in the atmosphere began to change. Suddenly the night grew darker. The streetlights flickered. A cool breeze shot through the warm summer air. The noisy streets were now quiet. And then the music started. It was far away, but Dac could still hear it. He rushed to Quentin's side.

"Take these," he said as he handed Quentin a pair of earplugs.

Quentin put the earplugs in his ears. They both looked at each other, knowing the situation was getting serious. Then the realization came, and they understood the music was coming from the direction of their house. Dac quickly grabbed the phone in his pocket. He called Emmaline's line and told her to find Nikolai and make sure the two of them stayed downstairs. They wouldn't be affected by the music underground.

Quentin suggested they follow the sound, and Dac agreed. Luca would have to wait. Maybe they didn't need him after all. Whoever had the music box was already using it. All they had to do was follow it and find them. It was risky, Dac knew, but it was their best shot of saving their friend and themselves.

They removed the earplugs from their ears and listened carefully to the music playing, letting it pull them into a trance. They followed the sound as it led them not to another building but to their own house. And then the music stopped.

A car sped past them; its headlights turned off. Quentin chased after it, but even with his vampire speed, he couldn't catch whoever it was. He turned to Dac, who was already at the front steps of the house.

"It felt like something was protecting the car, preventing me from getting close to it. I don't understand. I should have been able to catch it." Quentin said as he reached their front door.

Dac looked at Quentin. "The hunter."

Dac reached out and turned the handle to the front door. He and Quentin entered the house to find Emmaline sitting on the stairs. She had her arms wrapped around her knees, and her head hung low. She gazed up at them when she heard them enter.

"Nikolai is gone." Tears streamed down Emmaline's face.

Without a word, Dac stormed back out of the house. The morning light was not far behind, but he didn't care. He sensed Emmaline and Quentin trailing behind him, but he didn't care about that either. He had one focus now, and that was to find Nikolai.

He crossed the city for the second time that night, finding himself back in the same area he and Quentin had left a few moments ago. He stood in front of a large multistory building, looking up into the long glass windows of an apartment on the 13th floor. There they were, Luca and Harper. Luca's arms wrapped around Harper, and her head rested against his shoulder as they stared back down at him.

Quentin and Emmaline came up behind him. They both stared up at the building. He knew they saw exactly what he saw. They both put a hand on each one of his shoulders. The heat inside him raged to the surface, warming his usual cold interior. He clenched his jaw, his fangs biting into his lower lip. It was then that he realized what he needed to do.

Twenty

Harper stared out the window across the dark city. Luca's arms wrapped tightly around her made her feel warm and secure. They had grown close over the past few days, and she loved how she could be herself with him. He encouraged her in ways others never had. He protected her without questions or threats.

As she glanced down towards the street, a dark shadow appeared. A figure stood on the sidewalk beneath them, glaring up towards the window. Harper focused her vision on Dac's familiar features, thankful for her vampiric senses. Two others joined him at that moment. She wanted to look away, but somehow, she couldn't. Somehow, she was transfixed on his eyes, holding his gaze until he suddenly turned around and walked away.

"He saw us, didn't he?" She turned to face Luca.

"Yea, but I don't think we have to worry about him tonight. The sun will be rising soon enough, and they have to get back to their home before that happens." He reassured her before adding. "We must go too."

Harper took one last look around the luxurious apartment before she and Luca walked out the door. Outside the window, the sky was beginning to show the colors of dawn. Within minutes the sun would be making its way above the horizon. She wished she could stand at those windows and watch the sunrise. Sunrises were just one of the things she took for granted as a human. Now, as a vampire, her life had so many restrictions, as she had to live in secret.

Luca placed his hand on her back and guided her out the door and into the elevator to the ground floor. From there, they made their way to the basement and through the tunnels to their secret storage room.

Harper lay on her single cot that Luca had gotten for her to sleep on, knowing she wasn't fond of coffins. She glanced at him in his coffin, wondering how he could look so peaceful. Her thoughts were scattered as the morning fatigue began to cloud her mind. She wondered how she managed to get herself into yet another mess. Once again, all she was trying to do was help a friend and, in the process, managed to make things worse.

Unable to rest, she sat up and looked around the dark room. A leather case on the floor caught her eye. She got up to retrieve it. She flipped open the gold latches and opened the case. It was packed with kitchen cutlery. She looked at the varied sizes of knives laid out against the felt interior. She picked up one of the knives by its wooden handle and pressed her fingertip against the sharp point at the end of the blade. A small drop of blood appeared and slid down the blade. She sat back on her cot, knife still in hand. She hadn't thought of cutting herself since that last incident, but now here she was staring into the silver blade at her reflection, feeling the urge to swipe its rigged edge against her flesh. Instead, she dropped the knife to the floor and lay down. She stared at the dark ceiling until her eyes finally closed, allowing her to give in to the weakness her body felt, and she fell asleep.

The hours of sleep were more peaceful than she imagined they'd be. When she opened her eyes, Luca was sitting up in the chair, holding the knife in his hand. Harper recognized it as the one she had dropped on the floor earlier that morning. He was twirling the knife skillfully between his fingers, then he stood up, tossed it onto the chair cushion, and walked out of the room without saying a word. Harper sat there for a moment staring at the knife that still contained remnants of her blood. She ran to the open door. Luca was already halfway down the corridor. She looked back at the knife one more time before stepping out into the hall and closing the door tight behind her.

She raced through the tunnel to catch up to Luca, never quite reaching him. For the first time, she was in the building lobby alone. Without Luca by her side, she felt exposed and vulnerable. She walked briskly towards the elevators with her head down. She rode the elevator to the 13th floor. The apartment door was open. She figured Luca must be waiting for her. But as she stepped in through the threshold, her eyes grew wide. She swallowed hard and pulled in a deep breath, trying to quell her surprise. The one waiting in the apartment was not Luca.

"What are you doing here?" Harper demanded. Seeing Dac sitting on Luca's couch, one leg crossed over the other, her heart was racing, but she wasn't going to show him that she was afraid.

"I am looking for my brother. Where is he?"

"I don't know," Harper answered, keeping her tone neutral.

"Don't lie to me, Harper. I know you two have gotten close. Where is he?"

"I told you I don't know."

"Look, I'm not here to hurt either of you. I just need to speak with my brother, so if you could please stop trying to be a hero and tell me where he is."

"Again, I do not know. As you see, I just got here myself." Her patience was wearing thin with his insistence that she knew where Luca was when in fact, she had been searching for him herself.

"Listen to me, Harper. Nikolai is gone. Whatever our differences are right now, we need to work together to find him. Now, where is Luca." Dac uncrossed his legs and sat up straight.

"I don't know," Harper screamed before calming herself and finally saying, "But I might have an idea. Stay here. I'll go look for him."

"No need. I'm right here." They both turn to see Luca standing in the doorway. "So, I see my brother has come asking for my help." Luca turned his attention towards Dac, who had made himself a bit too comfortable in his apartment. "Why should I help you now after you so blatantly turned down my help before?" He asked.

"I realize you may not care what happens to Nikolai, but I know Harper does, and I know the two of you have gotten close, so if not to help me, do it for her."

"I warned you about Alex, and now look. Just as I've said"

"It wasn't Alex. It was the hunter, Brigid." Dac shifted in his seat.

"Ha ha ha," Luca laughed out loud. "Wouldn't she be like 90 years old by now? I seriously doubt she took your friend."

"She has help, obviously. And I'm pretty sure one of those people helping her is your friend Jace." Dac said, turning his attention towards Harper.

"Well, maybe had you not frightened him and tried to kill him, he wouldn't have turned to those vampire hunters for help. Had you just let him be and do as I asked him to do, then maybe we wouldn't be in this predicament." Luca walked over to the window and looked outside at the flickering lights of the city below.

"Jace was helping you, and now he's working with the hunter?" Dac grimaced. "So, how did you let him escape after you took him from my house?"

"I advised him to stay here, of course," Luca turned back around to face Dac, who was now standing. "Mostly for his safety from you, but unlike you, I wasn't keeping him prisoner. Now go home. I'll come to you when I'm ready." Luca was authoritative as he commanded his younger brother to leave his residence.

Harper watched Dac leave the apartment. Her heart sank with the realization that Nikolai was in trouble and that Jace was the one who had him. They were supposed to be working together, but she hadn't expected things to go this far this soon. What was Alex planning, she wondered? Would Jace be able to keep Nikolai safe long enough for her and Luca to get there? Also, did Alex really know who killed Cloe? Would Jace still care about protecting Nikolai once he got this information? The tears began to form in her eyes, and she blinked them away. She turned her head to face Luca. He was staring down at her.

"We should go find Jace." She said to him.

"We will. I'm sure your friend is fine for now. First, we need to talk."

"About the knife?" She turned her head slightly away from him and fixed her eyes towards the floor. She knew this moment would come since he had left her earlier.

"Yes, about the knife. What are you doing, Harper?" Luca reached out and gently placed his hands on each of her arms.

"It's really not a big deal. I don't even do it that much anymore." Harper turned away from him and sat down on the sofa.

"Anymore? How long have you been doing this? Did you do it when you were human?"

"No, just since after Noxwood. I don't even know how it started. I guess I just feel so overwhelmed sometimes. It just helps me release."

"I'm sorry," he said to her as he sat next to her on the sofa. "I never should have let Alex drag you into all of this. And I wasn't very kind to you in the beginning."

"It's fine. We didn't know each other then, not like we do now. I was just a girl who looked like Una, and you were just Dac's evil brother."

"Dac's evil brother," Luca repeated as he laughed. "Please promise me something. Whenever you're feeling overwhelmed, you'll come talk to me. Ok?"

"I promise." She focused her eyes on his though she kept her head held down.

"Good. Now let's go see Jace and meet these vampire hunters. Are you ready for this?" Harper nodded. Luca took her hand and led her out of the apartment and outside into the warm summer night.

Before making the trip to Aura Springs, Luca told Harper she needed to feed first. Deciding they didn't have much time to hunt, they chose instead to stop by Dac's blood bank. When they got to the building, it was closed up as expected. Harper had the code to unlock the door, which she punched into the keypad. They stepped into the clinic, making their way through the dark halls to where the blood was kept. Harper took a container filled with blood and drank it down.

"This really is a good idea," Luca said, and Harper looked at him sideways. Knowing how he liked the thrill of the hunt and the experience one felt from drinking from a living being, she was surprised to hear him say that. But she had to admit it was a good idea to keep blood on the ready.

Minutes later, they were on their way to Aura Springs to find Jace, Sarah, and her grandmother, and hopefully Nikolai.

WHEN THEY GOT CLOSE to Sarah's house, they could hear Jace talking to someone. "I'm not giving him to you until you tell me who killed Cloe. That was the deal." They heard him say. It was clear he was talking to Alex. Harper was relieved, knowing that, at least for now, Nikolai was ok. But how long would he stay that way? Jace was taking a chance talking to Alex that way. Alex could kill him before he even had a chance to defend himself and just take Nikolai. Unless Jace wasn't keeping Nikolai at this house, and Alex didn't know where he was. Also, she was sure the vampire hunters would have given Jace something to protect himself.

She opened her mouth to ask Luca what they should do, but he motioned for her to stay quiet. They crept up to the side of the house, being extra careful not to be noticed. They listened to the argument between Alex and Jace. Alex was demanding he turn Nikolai over to him, but Jace was holding his ground, even against Alex's threats. It was clear that Jace knew he had the upper hand. At least for now. Alex finally relented and backed off. He promised he'd be back with the information Jace wanted and told Jace he better have both Nikolai and Dac by the time he came back.

Luca made a move as if he were going to advance on Alex, but he was gone before Luca could reach him. Jace turned to look in Luca's direction, and Luca ducked back out of sight.

At that same moment, Harper started to move away from her hiding spot, but Luca held her back. "Wait," he whispered. "I want to see what he says to the other two first." Harper stepped back and crouched back down against the side of the house. Moments later, they heard the sliding door open and close. Jace went inside the house. Using their vampiric hearing, they listened in on the conversation happening on the other side of the wall.

Inside the house, Jace wasn't saying much more than he had said outside to Alex. There was only one other voice besides Jace's. That voice belonged to Sarah. She seemed to be in agreement that they shouldn't do anything further until Alex or even Luca held up their end of the deal made between Jace and either Vampire. They agreed as long as they had Nikolai, they had the advantage.

Harper turned to Luca. "Let me talk to him," she said. Luca nodded, and Harper quickly made her way to knock on the door before Luca could change his mind. Sarah answered and turned to Jace, who nodded to let Harper in.

"Where's Luca?" Jace asked. "You know Alex was just here."

"We saw him just as we got here, so we waited. Luca is right outside. I wanted to talk to you alone."

"Alone? Why? So, you can try convincing me to let your friend go." Jace's voice was full of contempt.

Harper thought for a moment before responding. She needed to choose her words carefully if she was going to get what she wanted. They had been friends not too long ago, but something had changed in Jace within the last few days. Jace was after only one thing, and that was something she couldn't let happen. She had given him the dagger so he could protect himself against any vampire that might be after him, like Dac or even Alex, who she definitely didn't trust. But she couldn't allow him to continue this hunt for the vampire he was determined to find. That, she knew, would not end well for anyone. She needed to put a stop to all of this.

"No, I'm not going to ask you to let him go. Not yet anyway. We all agreed to work together, right? So, let's do that. In the meantime, I'm only going to ask that I can see Nikolai. I just need to see that he's ok."

"Of course, he's fine, Harper. Do you really think I would do anything to him? Luca said to do whatever Alex asked, so I did. Now that you two are here, maybe one of you can tell me what's the next part of the plan. Just don't expect me to hand over Nikolai, or even Alex for that matter, until someone tells me who killed Cloe. And I don't know why you're not more concerned about that. She was your best friend once." Jace walked over to the sliding glass door at the back of the house. He peaked his head out the door, looking for Luca, who he found seated in a chair on the back porch.

Now that Luca had joined them, Harper again decided to choose her next words carefully. At any minute, Luca would take control of the conversation, but she needed first to persuade Jace to stop his search and still continue to help them.

"She was my best friend, Jace, and of course, I wish I knew who killed her, but let us handle that. Take it from me, don't consume yourself with revenge. I'll make sure Cloe gets justice. Please, help us get to Alex, and then please go back to your life. Forget you ever knew any of us, and allow yourself to heal."

"What do you want me to do?" Jace asked. It was a non-committal response, but Harper hoped she had gotten through to him.

"Next time Alex shows up here looking for where you've hidden Nikolai, give him this," Luca passed Jace a piece of paper with an address written on it. "Soon as he leaves, call this number." He handed him another paper. "We'll be there waiting for him." Luca then grabbed Harper by the hand, and the two of them were gone before Jace could refuse.

"What about Nikolai?" Harper asked once they were back on the train to Aura City.

"There are other ways to find him, and you obviously have your reasons for not wanting Jace to know Cloe's killer, so he won't find out from me."

"Do you know who killed her? And what about Alex? If we can find Nikolai without Jace telling us, then couldn't he also?"

"To answer your first question, no, I don't know, but I won't go looking for the answer unless you ask me to. As for Alex, yes, he could find Nikolai on his own if he wanted to, but the thing to know about Alex is although he's dangerous because he's smart and cunning and full of hatred, he's also lazy. He'd rather not put in the work if someone else can do it for him."

"I see."

"But there's something else you should know too. Dac could find Nikolai on his own too. Him coming to us for help means he's up to something. Be careful."

Harper glared out the window. They kept silent the rest of the way home.

Twenty-One

The next few weeks had mainly gone by uneventfully. There was no word or sighting of any vampire. Jace spent a few hours a day at his office, and the rest of the time he and Sarah spent training as Brigid had instructed them to do. They went to the gym and took self-defense classes. Jace was now splitting his time between his own house and Sarah's, although he still spent most of his time at Sarah's. Being with Sarah and her grandmother and having something to focus on distracted him from his grief. He felt a familiar bond forming between them with each passing moment. They were becoming more than partners; they were becoming family. It was a connection he hadn't felt since Cloe and Harper.

Jace had grown up an only child to divorced parents. He spent the school months with his mother and the summers with his dad. He didn't have close family ties on either side. Throughout his life, his most intimate friends became his family. Although he had a cousin, Janice, who eventually moved to Aura Springs late last year, they were never very close. Though when he found out Harper's ex, Zaine, was hanging around her, he became protective and warned him to stay away. It didn't matter much since, not long after that, the vampires killed Zaine. Jace never did know which one killed him. Was it Luca or Alex? Remembering Zaine's mutilated body, he imagined it was most likely Alex, though, at the time, they had all suspected it was Luca. But now, after meeting Luca, Jace couldn't imagine Luca being so brutal. He knew he was dangerous. All vampires were dangerous, but Luca seemed so calm. The one who killed Zaine was an animal. Jace tried not to think of those days like he tried not to think of the day Cloe killed herself. But no matter how hard he tried, he couldn't push those images out of his head. That's why he was doing the things he was doing now. That's why he was training, and when the time came, he would destroy any vampire that got in his way. Cloe's death would be avenged, no matter what the cost.

Jace was at his house when Sarah called him and asked to meet him at her shop. He packed up his computer, poured his coffee into his thermos, and drove right over. The bells on top of the shop door jingled as he opened it and stepped inside. He was met with the scent of candle wax and incense. As many times as he had been to the shop, he never seemed prepared for the assault of mixed aromas.

He called out to Sarah when she didn't come out when the bells chimed. He looked around the small shop, checking her back room where she would meet with clients. It was quiet and empty. Her traditional music wasn't playing through the shop speakers. No customers were in the store, nor were there any outside on the sidewalk. Upon realizing this, he peeked his head out of the glass door. The bells chimed again. The only cars in the parking lot were his and Sarah's. Jace checked his watch. The time read quarter to five. Most of the stores in this area didn't close until at least eight o'clock.

He stepped back into the shop, making sure the door closed securely behind him this time. It was odd that everything seemed closed up. Could he have his days mixed up somehow? He checked the calendar on his cell phone. No, it was Friday. This was very odd indeed. He felt his mouth become dry and his muscles tighten. He thought about the vampires, but the sky was still too bright. Sundown was not for another few hours. He stood against the counter and looked down at his phone, tapping on the screen and getting ready to call Sarah, when he heard footsteps in the other room. He looked up, and there stood Sarah. Her face looked wary and tired. He could tell something was wrong.

"This was on the door this morning." She said to him as she handed him a white sheet of paper with printed lettering on it. Jace looked at the letter, reading the words typed out in black ink. It was a notice from the property management company of the building which housed Sarah's shop. The announcement was informing them of a construction project and telling the residents they would need to shut down their stores temporarily until the project was complete, starting immediately.

"I came in just before dawn this morning and found these notices taped to everyone's doors," Sarah continued when she noticed Jace had finished reading the note. "It was way so early, and them giving no notice seemed suspicious to me. I waited until the other store owners arrived this morning, and after talking with a few of them, we decided to call the management company to confirm the validity of the notice. They confirmed they had not sent it and that there is no scheduled construction at this time but advised that we all vacate the premise until they can investigate the issue."

"You think it's the vampires? You think they figured Nikolai is being kept here?" Jace asked.

"Don't you?"

"Yea, I do." Jace let out a deep sigh.

"I checked on Nikolai," Sarah reassured him. "He's still here. So, either it was too close to daylight, and they plan on coming back tonight, or they have some other plan in mind. Either way, we need to move him before it gets dark. I talked to my grandmother. She made arraignments to have him transported. Apparently, she has an old friend who was willing to help."

"More vampire hunters?" Jace was nervous about letting anyone else in on the plan.

"No, just someone willing to do her a favor, no questions asked, but that's why I need your help now instead of just telling you all this later," Sarah told him.

"So, what's the plan? Where are we moving him?"

"We need to wrap him up and make it not look like a body," Sarah instructed. "This guy will be here soon and take him for us. He'll be safe."

"And where will he be?" Jace asked again.

"In a locked drawer at the morgue."

"What!?"

Sarah explained, as Brigid had explained to her earlier, that Nikolai is a vampire and therefore immortal. The morgue was the safest place to store him until their own demands were met. In any other site, the other vampires would be able to find him eventually, just as they had this time. It was pure luck they had not found him sooner. Probably because Nikolai was not fully healed from his last injuries. Although he looked healed physically, it was clear that his full strength and power had not yet been restored. Otherwise, it would not have been so easy to take him in the first place. At least at the morgue, there would be no chances of daylight reaching him, and locked inside that drawer, he would be in a constant sleep, unable to communicate telepathically with the other vampires.

Reluctantly Jace followed Sarah through the downstairs storage room. Behind the padlocked, white door lay a sleeping vampire. Sarah held the music box in her hands. As a precaution, she opened the lid, and the soft melody began to play. If Nikolai sensed them and awoke, the music would entrance him back into slumber.

Jace didn't like the idea of what they were doing, but nonetheless, he followed Sarah's lead as they placed Nikolai on a thick slab of wood and fitted pieces of cardboard around him, then wrapped his body in thick paper and packing tape like a Christmas present. All that was missing was the printed gift wrap and a pretty bow. Not long after they had finished, a knock was heard at the top of the steps. A man's voice called down to them.

The man came down the stairs and introduced himself as the person Brigid said would be coming to retrieve Nikolai. Looking at the package, he decided he would drive his truck around to the loading dock outside the basement storage room. Moments later, the man appeared at the storage room door that led to the outside loading dock. Jace helped him load Nikolai into the white van and then watched as he drove away. Sarah put a hand on his shoulder. "He'll be fine," She assured him. "Remember, the vampires are not your friends. They never were. There'll come a time when the choice will be you or them. When that time comes, Jace, who will it be? Are you sure you're ready for this?"

Jace nodded. "Yea, I'm ready," he said, although he wasn't sure he was.

The stress of the day had Jace feeling like he needed a break. He stepped outside of Sarah's shop. The sun was descending in the sky, though Jace determined they still had another hour or two before complete sundown. He pulled his cellphone from his pocket and dialed Alan's number, sending him a text to meet at the bar. Behind him, the bells chimed as Sarah exited the Shop. He turned to face her. She had her back to him, locking the door.

"I'm going to meet Alan. You wanna come?" Jace asked Sarah.

"Sure." She shrugged. She lifted her bag higher on her shoulder. They each walked to their respective cars. Jace drove his car out of the parking lot first, and Sarah followed behind him.

At the bar, Alan was already waiting, seated at a table in the far corner. Jace and Sarah joined him. They ordered drinks, and over the next few hours, they laughed and joked. There was no talk of vampires or the supernatural, and for a while, everything felt normal. But outside, the evening sky was growing darker. Jace couldn't help periodically glancing out the far window, and he noticed Sarah did the same.

Eventually, Alan stood up to leave. He said goodbye to both Jace and Sarah, leaving them alone at the table. They each ordered one more drink, not quite ready to call it a night. The minutes passed in silence while they consumed their last drinks. The music that would normally play over the bar's speaker system seemed to have stopped. Jace watched Sarah stir the ice around in her glass with the thin red and white striped straw. He wondered what she was thinking but feared her answer. Instead, he excused himself to the restroom.

He stood in front of the sink and turned on the faucet. He cupped his hands under the running water, splashing his face with water and then patting himself dry with the rough paper towels. With his hands resting on the laminate countertop, he leaned forward towards the vanity mirror. The bloodshot eyes that stared back at him revealed his exhaustion. The muscles in his shoulders tightened. He straightened up, dropped the crumpled-up paper towel he still grasped in his hand into the wastebasket, and walked back out into the bar. When he reached the table, he tapped on the back of Sarah's chair. "You ready to go?" He asked. She nodded and grabbed her bag. Jace paid the tab and met her outside where they had parked their cars. Jace wanted to spend the night alone in his own home, so they agreed to meet the next morning at Sarah's house.

In his bedroom, Jace lay on his bed staring at the ceiling. The bright light from the ceiling lamp above him burned his eyes, but he couldn't bring himself to turn it off. He thought of himself and Sarah wrapping up Nikolai's sleeping vampire corpse and the vampire now being stored in a drawer in the morgue. What if the vampire woke up? Would he be scared? Confused? Would he find a way to escape and come after them? Sarah assured him that he wouldn't awaken, nor would he be able to escape if somehow, he did wake up, but Jace wasn't convinced. With the room spinning, like the thoughts in his head, he closed his eyes and fell into a light, dreamless sleep.

Twenty-Two

Jace arrived the next morning at Sarah's house as promised. He knocked a few times before she answered the door. Although, he knew she was awake because he could hear her and her grandmother inside. Sarah had a look of irritation on her face when she greeted Jace at the door. She tried to hide it with a smile as she invited him inside, though Jace could see she was clearly angry about something. She asked him to wait in the living room, and she went back to the kitchen to continue the conversation she'd been having with her grandmother.

Jace could smell the coffee brewing in the other room. His mouth started to water with the aroma creeping up his nostrils. The smell was so strong he could almost taste it. He sat patiently while he waited for Sarah and Brigid to join him. He wasn't sure what they were discussing, but he could tell it was contentious. Then he heard Brigid say, "When the time comes, you need to be able to do what he will not." Sarah tried defending Jace, but Brigid hushed her. "You will understand soon enough," was all she said. Jace wondered what she meant by that. Then he heard their footsteps coming from the kitchen into the living room where he had been waiting for them. He straightened up and greeted Brigid as she entered the room.

The smell of coffee and fresh-baked muffins filled the air. Sarah walked in carrying a tray with the food and drinks. She placed it on the coffee table and took a seat on the couch next to Jace. Brigid sat on the oversized plush chair, resting her cane against the arm. Sarah handed her grandmother a mug of coffee and then took one for herself. Jace picked up the third mug, thankful for its warm contents. Although it was a hot summer morning, the warm coffee and muffins eased his rumbling stomach.

While the three of them sat and ate breakfast, they talked about the next steps they'd need to take against the vampires. It wouldn't be long before Alex showed up looking for Nikolai, and now, he added Dac to the deal. Brigid was confident there was more to it now than just getting revenge on the father who abandoned him. He wanted something more. But what was it?

Luca and Harper would be back soon looking for Nikolai also. Jace had succeeded in holding them off for now, but for how long? Not to mention Dac. It was only a matter of time before he and the other two showed up. Jace was surprised they hadn't already. The most concerning thing, however, was that one of them knew that Nikolai had been being held below Sarah's store, and it was very likely they knew by now that he was no longer there. So, what were they going to do? Jace was clear they were not handing Nikolai over to anyone until he found out who killed Cloe. Sarah and Brigid agreed.

Sarah reminded Jace of the address, and phone number Luca handed to him the other night. He had said to tell Alex that is where Nikolai would be and to contact him as soon as Alex was given the address. Brigid agreed this would be a good plan to get them all in one place. Luca could destroy Alex for them, but Jace reminded her that Luca wouldn't do that. He still owed his life to Alex for rescuing him from the grave that Nikolai and Dac had put him in. That gave Sarah an idea, though.

"What if you contact Dac and make the same deal with him?" Sarah suggested. Jace and Brigid looked at her. "You could tell Dac if he gets you the name of Cloe's killer, you'll give him Nikolai's location. Once Alex comes, you give him Luca's address. When you contact Luca, you also contact Dac. They all show up. Dac has no reason not to kill Alex." She continued.

"Except that he's Nikolai's son." Jace countered.

"Yea, but from what you've told me of them, I think Dac would protect Nikolai over sparing his son's life."

"You might be right," Jace said. Brigid agreed it was a good plan.

Brigid wanted Sarah to do some private training on her own, so Jace went back home to get a few work things done. He figured he'd be taking some more days off soon, and he didn't want to leave too much on Alan's plate. While he worked on his laptop, he found it hard to concentrate. The conversation he overheard between Sarah and Brigid replayed in his mind. It was obvious to him that the conversation had to do with the private training Brigid wanted Sarah to do. They weren't exactly secretive about it, but they weren't forthcoming either. Jace couldn't help wondering what exactly it was Brigid was concerned he couldn't or wouldn't do.

Unable to focus any longer on his work, Jace closed his laptop and began pacing around his house. He grew more and more restless and anxious. He looked at the clock on the wall. It was now late afternoon. He checked his phone. No calls had come in from Sarah or anyone else. He put his phone down and picked it back up again, tapping the screen to bring it to life. He swiped through the screens staring at the many apps though not clicking on any of them. Finally, he clicked on the messaging icon, ready to type a message to Sarah, when something on the floor caught his eye. It was a white business card with the name and phone number of the guy that helped them with Nikolai yesterday. This gave Jace an idea. He called the number on the card. When the man answered, Jace asked if he could check on the package he had stored for him and Sarah a day earlier. He agreed to meet Jace at the morgue so that he could check on Nikolai.

Jace pulled up to the yellow building. The man was standing in the parking lot, leaning against the side of his car. He had a cigarette in his hand, which he tossed to the ground and stomped out as soon as Jace approached him. He led Jace to the side of the building and unlocked the door. He pulled on the large metal handle opening the door. Jace followed the man through the hall into a concrete room. Jace covered his mouth and nose with his shirt. A body was on a tray covered in a white sheet. Its feet hung out the end covered in blue and reddish blemishes that the man called death's bruises. He explained to Jace that this happens when the cells of the body stop working and the blood rushes to the lowest point.

To the right of him, the wall was lined with steel drawers. The man walked over to the last row of drawers and opened the one at the very bottom corner. Jace shivered as he looked in on the still wrapped body of a vampire he once thought of as a friend. Satisfied the vampire was safe, he motioned for the man to close the draw and quickly left the building.

There were still a few hours left until dusk. Jace would need to find something to do until then. He intended to go to the vampire house tonight and speak with Dac. He knew it was risky, but he had the one thing that would make Dac listen, and that was Nikolai.

While he waited, he went to the gym to work off some of his nervous energy. Afterward, he went home, showered, and prepared himself for his visit to the vampire house. When he had been captured by Quentin, they had taken his oils and the cross necklace he wore around his neck, but since then, Sarah had mixed him new oils, which he placed in his pockets now. He rubbed the cream Brigid had given him into the skin of his temples, neck, and wrists as usual. As he was putting the jars away, he noticed the stone pendant Brigid had given him when they had first met. He must not have been wearing it the night he met with Una, and then Quentin took him captive. The stones inside the pendant were supposed to keep him protected from harm. He placed the necklace around his neck and tucked the pendant under his shirt.

Dusk was finally approaching. While Jace was driving, he pulled on his sunglasses and lowered the visor to repel the bright glare of the evening sun as it lowered itself into the sky. It would be just turning dark when he reached the vampire house. He'd park his car in his usual spot and waited for the perfect moment to approach. He noticed a light go on through one of the front windows. He decided it was time.

As he had hoped, Emmaline answered the door. A look of worry and confusion crossed her face. Jace sensed her concern when she asked why he was there.

"Hi," he said. "Can you speak to Dac, ask him to speak with me?"

"I don't think that's a good idea, Jace. You shouldn't even be here. He'll kill you on sight." Emmaline pretested, but her voice remained soft.

"I don't think he will. I have something he wants, and if he can get me what I want, he can have it back."

"Nikolai!" Emmaline raised her voice. "Jace, what are you doing? I thought we were friends. Why are you working with those hunters?"

"I thought we were friends too, but then you refused to help me. Dac and Quentin tried to kill me, and all I want to know is who killed my fiancée. Now please, can you get Dac for me?" Jace pleaded with her.

Emmaline relented. She led him into the front room, the same one she had on the first night he had come to this house when Harper had sent him. She told him to wait while she went upstairs to find Dac. He and Quentin were in his office.

Moments later Dac entered the room. His expression was neutral, but his dark eyes pierced into Jace's as if reaching down and touching the core of his soul. Jace stood, straightening his posture to match Dac's height.

"I'm here to make a deal," he stated, doing his best to keep his tone even.

Dac sat in one of the chairs and gestured for Jace to do the same. Jace followed suit sitting in the chair across from him. He kept both feet planted firmly on the ground. He folded his hands in front of him and leaned his body forward.

"As I'm sure you've guessed by now, I have Nikolai. He is safe for now." Jace watched Dac's eyes narrow, and then he continued. "All I want is the name and location of the vampire that killed my fiancée, Cloe. After that you can have your friend back unharmed. You will also receive the whereabouts of Alex and your brother Luca."

"Well, I already know where my brother is, and he informed me you were working for him. You see, so you've already lost one of your bargaining chips. But we have agreed to work together, for the time being, he and I, so I'll tell you what, since I don't trust him, I'll agree to your terms."

"Great," Jace said with a little too much enthusiasm. He corrected his tone as he spoke the next sentences. "Here's how this is going to work. Alex is going to come to me looking for you and Nikolai."

"Me?" Dac interrupted.

"Yes. Alex wants you both in exchange for the same information I asked of you."

"I see, so you are double-crossing both him and my brother. Clever. Stupid, but clever."

Jace ignored that comment and continued detailing the plan to Dac. "When Alex contacts me again, I will give him Nikolai's location. I will contact you in the meantime so you can show up when he does. You can do with Alex what you will and take Nikolai home with you. And as I said, all I want is the name and location of Cloe's killer. So, you better work fast because I have a feeling Alex will be showing up again soon. But I don't trust he will have the information for me. Neither do I believe your brother will."

"And you trust I will?"

"Yes, because the difference between you and the two of them is you actually care about what happens to Nikolai."

"You are correct about that," Dac said as he stood from his chair. "Fine, we have a deal. I'll wait for your call, and when I hear from you next, you'll have the information you're after." Dac walked over to a table in the corner and wrote something down on a small notepad. He tore out the page and handed it to Jace.

Jace looked at the paper with the number on it, folded it in half, and stuffed it in his pocket. He nodded to Dac and left out of the front door. Without looking back, he ran down the block to where he had parked his car. Once he was safely in his vehicle, he breathed a sigh of relief and drove home.

Twenty-Three

D ac stood in the doorway of what used to be Harper's room. All of her things were still there, although she was someplace else. So much had changed in less than a year. His most treasured relationships had both crumbled to nonexistent. And for that, he blamed his brother, Luca.

He stepped into the room, looking through Harper's things. He searched all the drawers and under the mattress, any place she may have kept a journal but found nothing. Harper hadn't talked much about her life as a human. He knew Cloe had been her close friend, but beyond that, he knew little about her. He was hoping Harper would have kept a journal describing that friendship. He was searching for anything that would give him a look inside that girl's life, looking for any reason her paths would have crossed with a vampire. He admitted it could have very well been coincidental, but if he were, to be honest, the timing did seem a bit off.

He sat on the floor of Harper's room, his back against the bed post, trying to think back over the last few years. Could Harper have been revealing herself to Cloe as she had with Zaine? If she had, that could have brought Cloe into the other vampire's sights. Or had it been about Jace? They knew Jace had been working with them. Una came to Jace pretending to be Harper. Could it have been Una? That would be the most logical choice. He needed to talk with his brother again and find out what happened after that night at his house after Alex had fled. He didn't like thinking about that night. That was the night everything changed for him.

It was the first time he had seen Luca after learning he was alive. He expected his brother wanted revenge for him and Nikolai trying to kill him. What he hadn't expected was for Nikolai's wife and son to have survived. All that time, they watched and waited for the opportunity to take down Luca. Not once had they seen any indication that Una was not only alive but had given birth to a son and become a vampire. But there they both were that night, and it had become apparent that Luca had not been the one seeking revenge, but it had been Una and Alex. However, Luca had for certain reveled in the truth of Dac's involvement in Una's kidnapping coming out. And for that, Dac would not forgive him. Luca claimed he wanted to protect him, that he wished to maintain a brotherly relationship, but he continued to destroy and take away the relationships Dac cherished most.

After Luca had locked him and Quentin in that room, the two of them watched as Alex revealed himself in a staged event of Una's killing. Quentin had sensed there was more to the story, and Dac had been harboring some type of secret. He forced Dac to tell him the truth, to reveal the part he played in the events of that original night. Once he did, Quentin drained his energy so that he couldn't follow him down to the room where Nikolai was, but Dac watched through the glass window as Quentin appeared just in time to catch Alex before he stabbed Nikolai with the dagger that he pulled from inside his jacket.

Quentin and Alex struggled, each trying to gain control over the other. That's when Dac saw her appear behind where Nikolai stood. The one with the long dark hair and pale skin. The one who shared a face with Harper. Una and Dac locked eyes. She saw him too. She winked at him and flashed her pearly white fangs. Then Dac saw the knife in her hand. The one she had pressed against Nikolai's back. He saw her whisper something in Nikolai's ear. He banged furiously on the glass window separating him from the others. Finally, he backed up to the other side of the room. With all the strength he could gather, he thrust forward, his shoulder shattering the glass into tiny fragments as he crashed through the window. Twinkling shards floated through the air before falling to the ground underneath him.

Dac landed on his feet, knees crouched, his hands hit the ground. Broken glass pierced through the flesh of his palms. His eyes darted up to look in Nikolai's direction. He was too late. Una had pierced the knife through his back. The long blade extending through the other side of his torso. Blood spilled rapidly to the floor. He rushed over to his friend, whose body had fallen hard to the ground. He glanced around the room as he cradled Nikolai in his arms. Una and Alex were nowhere to be seen.

He pulled the knife out from Nikolai's back and wrapped his shirt tightly around the gaping wound. Quentin rushed over, transferring some of his energy into Nikolai in an attempt to save his friends life. As Dac attempted to carry Nikolai out of the house, Luca came up in front of him. His wings expanded. "Let me take him to your home. I can get him there faster than you," Luca had offered.

Quentin stared at Dac with a look of disdain and distrust, then turning away from him, Quentin released Harper from her chains and carried her away to the car. Dac didn't follow. When he returned to the house they had been hiding out in, he overheard Quentin making arrangements to get himself and Harper back home to Aura City. They left the next evening, and Dac stayed behind. That was until recently, when Luca had warned him of Alex's disappearance.

Now he had to find Alex before he could cause any more damage, and it seemed the way to do that was by partnering up with Jace, the once vampire friend now turned vampire hunter. Sadly, he would have to deal with Jace eventually, but for now, he would give him what he wanted. He'd let him take out a few troublesome vampires and dispense of him later.

A few doors down, he heard Emmaline enter her room. This gave him an idea. He would ask her to talk with Jace. If anyone could get information out of him, it would be her. Of all the vampires, Jace trusted her the most, maybe even more than he did Harper. It hadn't gone unnoticed that during the time Jace had spent in the house, he and Emmaline had formed a sort of friendship. He checked the time. The summer didn't leave many dark hours, but it was early enough for her to get to Aura Springs, speak with Jace, and return home before sunrise.

THE COLD TEMPERATURE inside the Aura Springs Café was a welcoming contrast to the warm summer air outside. Jace stood at the counter waiting for his takeout order, sipping coffee from a paper cup. The Café was nearly empty, so when he heard someone call his name and realized it was his cousin Janice, he was surprised he hadn't noticed her when he walked in. He was also surprised to see that she was sitting there with his friend and business partner, Alan. He walked over to their table and sat when they offered him a seat. They chatted for a while, Jace trying his best to keep the conversation focused on the two of them. When the waitress brought over Jace's take-out order, he graciously excused himself and left the cafe.

Out in the parking lot, the air was thick and humid. As he reached for the doorhandle on his car, a cold touch covered his hand. A shadow loomed behind him. He froze in place, trying to steady his breath and keep his knees from buckling beneath him. A soft familiar voice spoke to him then, and the floral scent of Emmaline's heavy perfume calmed his nerves. Confident she wasn't here to harm him, Jace turned to face his former vampire friend.

"Can we go someplace to talk?" She asked him.

"Yea, I was just heading home. Get in." Jace gestured towards the car. He got in on the driver's side as Emmaline walked to the other side and got in the car. They drove mostly in silence to Jace's house. Emmaline tried to engage him in small talk, but Jace only gave short one-worded responses to her statements.

When they arrived at his house, Jace removed the hawthorn branches that hung from his front door before inviting Emmaline inside. He noticed her careful steps through his house as he led her into the living room. They both sat on his couch. Jace rested his elbows on his knees. The silence between them was awkward. He knew she was there for a reason, but what that reason was, he was not sure. He waited for her to speak, and once she finally did, it was not what he expected.

"Tell me about Cloe. What was she like?" Emmaline spoke in soft, comforting tones.

"Oh, you want to know about Cloe?" Jace couldn't help feeling a bit suspicious of her questions.

"Yea. Had she ever mentioned any strange occurrences or seeing anyone out of the ordinary? You know, someone that looking back knowing what you know now could be described as a vampire." Her questions felt a bit like an interrogation, but Jace let her continue. "Did she believe in the supernatural? Dac thinks it will help to find her killer if we know a little bit about her. He says that if we know a little about what she was like and places she went to, maybe it could help determine how she could have possibly gotten in the sights of a vampire."

"Or maybe it's one you already know," Jace suggested.

"Well, it wasn't one of us, and I think you know that, or you wouldn't have come to us for help, and Dac doesn't believe it was any of Luca's people because they were all in Noxwood by then." Emmaline's voice became defensive.

Jace wanted to believe Emmaline that it wouldn't have been one of them. What reason would they have had? He thought at the time they had reached some level of trust or friendship, but Brigid's words remained in the back of his mind. *The vampires are not your friends; they never were.* Still, he didn't want to believe they would have killed Cloe. They didn't even drink from humans, as far as he knew. And what she said about Luca and his crew of vampires made sense. Even if they wanted some type of revenge on him for helping Dac and Nikolai, they were all the way in Noxwood. Would they have risked coming back to Aura Springs just for that? And if they had, why would Alex and Luca both have agreed to help him. After giving some thought to Emmaline's request, Jace decided to provide her with the information she was looking for. What harm could it do at this point anyway? So, he told her Cloe's story starting from just after Harper's disappearance up until Cloe's death.

Twenty-Four

Cloe was by no means tall, standing just around five feet, but whenever she walked into a room, her presence demanded attention. Jace stood in front of the reception hall and watched Cloe command her assistants as they took down the decorations and began their clean-up. Silver table clothes still covered the tables. Red and pink roses in crystal vases stood as the center pieces. It must have been a beautiful event, as all her events were. She smiled at Jace when she finally noticed him standing in the doorway. She rarely smiled in those days, but when she did, her smile could still light up a room.

Cloe finished folding up the last table before walking over to where Jace stood in the doorway. "Hey." She glanced upwards to meet his eye.

"Hi." He looked down at her, unsure if she could see the sadness and anxiety in his eyes, knowing he couldn't hide it. "I wanted to talk to you before you heard it from somewhere else." He had said.

"What is it?" Her voice wavered.

"They found Zaine's car at the bottom of some lake or something, not far from his apartment. There's still no sign of Harper. He's saying he was alone and drunk, but I don't know. Something still doesn't sit right with me about all this."

"You think she was in the car, don't you?"

"I'm sorry. I definitely think he did something to her. Maybe he dumped her somewhere else and then dumped the car."

"I hate to admit it, but I think you might be right. Something is definitely not right. Harper wouldn't just disappear on her own like this." Cloe began twirling the ring she wore on her middle finger. Jace

163

put his arm around her and walked her outside to her car. The two of them agreed to meet at Cloe's apartment, where Jace had spent most of his time in the days following Harper's disappearance.

As the months and years passed after that night, Cloe and Jace had come to accept they might never know what happened to Harper. Eventually, life went back to normal. The couple got engaged. Jace bought a house. They were happy, though Cloe never forgot her best friend, and neither had Jace. The three of them had become quite close over the years since Harper had moved in down the hall from Cloe. It was only after Jace learned the truth about Harper's disappearance that everything had truly changed.

Jace kept the vampires' secret even after he and Emmaline had parted ways that last night at the Aura City train station. He locked away any evidence of their existence in a box and stored it atop the closet shelf, determined to put it all behind him. But even after he had come back home and he and Cloe were getting back on track, planning the wedding and their life together, Jace could sense something had changed in Cloe.

Winter was finally coming to an end. The temperature outside was starting to warm up though there was still a bit of a chill to the morning air. Jace had the living room window open and could feel the cool breeze come through to the kitchen. Cloe had come into the kitchen while he was sitting at the table eating his cereal and sipping his cup of coffee. Her hair still mussed from sleep, she sauntered over to the back counter where the coffee pot was and poured herself a cup. The spoon clinked against the ceramic mug when she stirred in the creamer and sugar. The smell of French Vanilla filled the room.

Quietly she walked past Jace into the living room and sunk down onto the couch. She curled up in the corner seat with a small blanket over her lap and sipped her coffee while staring blankly at the opposite wall. Jace called out to her. "Hey, you ok?" he asked.

"Huh?" She turned her head in his direction. "Oh, yea, I'm fine," she said after a pause as if his words had finally reached her. The tone in her voice was quiet and sleepy.

"Maybe you should take the day off for yourself, get a little rest. You seem tired." Jace thought it was reasonable considering the amount of time she had been spending working and planning the wedding. But she snapped at him.

"I said I'm fine." She slammed her mug down onto the coffee table, stood up, and then stormed off into the room.

Moments later, Jace heard the shower water running in the bathroom. He finished the last bits of cereal in his bowl and drank the remainder of his coffee. He scribbled a note for Cloe and placed it next to the coffee pot knowing she'd go back for a second cup; then, he left for work.

Jace was sitting at his desk right about lunchtime when his phone pinged with a message. He smiled when he saw Cloe's name across the screen. She'd sent a pic of the note he'd left her with a smiley face and heart emoji. Another message came through right after that asking him to meet her for dinner at the hotel restaurant where she worked. He messaged her back that he'd meet her directly after work, and he worked the rest of the day feverishly, so there'd be no need to stay late.

With the days growing longer, it was still daylight when Jace left the office that evening, although the sun hung low enough in the sky that he had to shield his eyes from its ferocious glare. It was a short drive between the office and the hotel where Cloe worked, but with the traffic of rush hour, Jace was beginning to get nervous he would be late. Cloe had been so on edge earlier that morning, Jace didn't want to stress her more than she already was.

When he arrived at the hotel, he made his way directly to the restaurant and told the host he was there to meet Cloe. The host led Jace over to Cloe's table. To Jace's surprise, Cloe's mother was sitting there waiting. Her hair was pulled back into a sophisticated ponytail.

She wore a simple cardigan over her floral-patterned dress, and a single string of pearls hung around her neck. She looked up from the menu in her hands just as Jace approached the table.

"Hello, Jace. Have a seat," she gestured to the chair across from her. "Cloe should be here to join us shortly," she reassured him.

"Mrs. Rais, how are you? Cloe didn't mention you'd be here." Jace responded.

"I'm doing well, thanks. We wanted to meet up to go over the menu for the engagement party."

The engagement party was in two weeks, and the food and drink menu for the restaurant needed finalizing. They had decided to host the party at the hotel since Cloe had decided on another venue for the wedding ceremony and reception. She and her mother were taking care of the majority of the arraignments for both the engagement party and the wedding, but Jace tried to help out wherever he could.

Cloe did show up just moments later. The three of them chatted a while about the party plans while looking over the menu. The wait staff brought out a variety of items for them to taste, including desserts. After a couple of hours and much discussion, they finally decided on the perfect menu for the guests at their party. With everything seemingly in place, Cloe and Jace said goodnight to Mrs. Rais and agreed to meet each other back at Jace's house.

The sun had finally made its way under the horizon by the time Jace and Cloe stepped outside the lobby of the hotel and into the parking lot. The moon had now made its appearance in the darkened sky. Cloe made a comment about the chill in the air. Jace wrapped his arms around her as he walked her to her car though he hadn't felt the same chill. The temperature felt rather warm to him, but he could feel the coolness of Cloe's skin.

That night Cloe tossed and turned in a restless sleep. Jace could hear her voice calling out to someone, but she sounded far off in the distance. He tried to reach for her but found himself in a state of sleep paralysis. His arms and legs felt heavy. Every movement took all of his strength. No matter how far he reached out, he couldn't seem to reach Cloe. He struggled to wake as he helplessly listened to her cries, unsure if it was his nightmare or hers.

When he awoke the following morning, he found Cloe already awake and, in the kitchen, making breakfast. She turned and smiled at him when he entered the room. He hadn't bothered to ask her about the night before, not wanting to risk her good mood. He quieted the troubled voice in his head and shrugged the ordeal off as a simple bad dream. He poured himself a cup of coffee and refilled her cup while she finished cooking. They ate breakfast together in comfortable silence, sharing glances and soft smiles across the table.

The next two weeks leading up to the party went by primarily uneventful. Jace was spending a lot of time at work, and so was Cloe. The spring and summer months were the busiest for Cloe, and Jace wanted to have as many projects completed as possible before taking time off for the wedding.

It rained the entire day of the engagement party. Jace thought Cloe would have been upset, but she wasn't. Instead, she said it felt like a good omen, almost like a cleansing. It seemed odd since Cloe wasn't usually one to believe in luck, good or bad, but Jace went along with it. Learning the things he had learned in the recent past about the existence of vampires, he was more open to the idea of other supernatural occurrences. If she believed the rain was a sign of good fortune, who was he to disagree.

They both got ready for the party at Jace's house and agreed to drive to the hotel together. Jace got dressed in his navy-colored suit with no tie and the collar of his white shirt left unbuttoned. He sat on his couch, scrolling through his phone to pass the time while he waited for Cloe. When Cloe finally entered the room, she took his breath away. She stood at the edge of the hallway. The crystals on her strappy sandals sparkled against her tan skin. The one-shouldered sky-blue dress she wore draped elegantly around her, with the hem ending at the top of her heel. She wore long chandelier earrings that grazed the top of her shoulders and no necklace. Shimmering champagne-colored eye shadow was swept across her eyelids. She smiled at him and did a little twirl. Jace stood up, stuffed his phone inside his pocket, and took Cloe in his arms. He kissed her gently on the lips, and then the two of them left together for the party.

All of their guests were waiting inside the small hotel ballroom by the time they had arrived early that evening. The music was playing. People were dancing and mingling. Both of their families and friends were getting along. The night was looking to be a success. Not that Jace was worried. He had always gotten along with Cloe's family, and she his, but this was the first time many of them were meeting each other.

Jace was talking to Cloe's parents when he noticed someone at the door to the ballroom. He was certain everyone had arrived that was invited. He hadn't seen the person's face, but he glanced their long black hair. Politely, he excused himself and searched for Cloe.

"Did you see someone in the doorway just now?" He had asked when he found her.

"No, I didn't. Probably one of the hotel staff. I'll go check, make sure everything's okay." She left out the double doors down the hall in search of one of her coworkers.

Jace waited by the entrance for Cloe to return. It seemed she was taking a long time, but he figured she was talking with one of her friends from the hotel. He only hoped things were okay. He wanted everything to be perfect for her. She worked so hard on putting this party together. After waiting another five or so minutes and Cloe still hadn't returned, Jace decided to look for her.

The hotel hallways were quiet. The soles of his shoes click-clacked as he walked along the tiled floors. Jace stopped by the restaurant first and asked the hostess standing at the host stand if she'd seen Cloe. She hadn't. Next, he went by the front desk to ask the agent there. She said Cloe had stopped by a few moments ago, but she thought she was heading back to the ballroom. Jace thanked her. It was likely they'd probably just missed each other. He began heading back to the party when he got a sudden urge to check for Cloe in her office.

He took the elevator to the third floor. When he stepped out, he thought he saw a shadow against the wall but saw no one nearby. Jace stood near the elevator door for a moment, looking in both directions down the long corridor. Convinced he was letting his imagination get the best of him, he pushed down his anxiety and walked around the corner to Cloe's office. The hallway was unusually dark. Jace noticed all but a few lights were out. When he reached the room Cloe used for an office, he noticed the faint light coming through the space under the door.

He reached for the doorknob and thought he heard voices inside. He stopped himself from opening the door straight away. Instead, he put his ear to the door to hear inside. It was silent now. He tried the door handle. It was unlocked, so he knocked lightly as he gently pushed the door open.

Cloe was sitting at her desk with her head resting on her hands. Loose strands of her curly hair dangled in front of her face. No one else was in the room. He told himself the voices he heard must have been coming from the room next door. He walked over to Cloe and gently put a hand on her shoulder.

"Are you ok? What happened?" He felt her jump under his touch as he accidentally startled her.

"Oh my God. You scared me." Both her hands touched against her chest.

"Sorry. I just came to check on you when you didn't come back to the party." Jace took a small step back to give Cloe some space.

"Yea, sorry about that. I just needed a moment."

"Are you ok?"

"I'm fine. I was talking to Elena at the front desk and started to feel tired, so I came up here for a minute. Sorry. I should have texted you." She glanced up at him with angelic eyes. Her voice was soft and apologetic.

"It's all right. I just wanted to make sure you were ok. Did she say if someone was looking for you?" He stretched his arm out and gently rubbed her bare shoulder. She reached up and placed her hand on top of his.

"No one was looking for me. Must have just been someone passing by. Everything's good. Let's get back downstairs to the party before our guests start to wonder where we went." Cloe stood up, and Jace wrapped his arm around her waist as they walked back to the ballroom.

The rest of the night went by without incident. They danced and drank champagne, opened presents and ate cake. One by one, their guests left until they were the only two left in the ballroom. Jace held Cloe in his arms, and they slow danced as she hummed in his ear. Two days later, Cloe collapsed on Jace's living room floor, and their lives were forever changed.

Twenty-Five

T he bloodstains on her floor must mean something. According to Quentin, Harper had been different ever since returning from Noxwood. They all had. It was to be expected after all that had happened and had been revealed.

It disturbed him that she had never bothered to clean the stains. He knew they came from the cuts she made in her skin. He imagined her slicing through her flesh and watching the wounds heal as they would with any vampire. He pictured her staring at the stains left behind, which covered the floor. He imagined the frustration that must have grown inside her that drew her to cut her throat that night. The vision he relived over and over of her lying on this very floor, the blood pooling out of the vein in her neck, and Emmaline screaming for help while she tried to stop the blood flow hurt him to his very core. Maybe if he had done more to protect her, she wouldn't have turned on him.

Dac had been standing in the doorway staring into Harper's empty room when Emmaline tapped his shoulder. Her cold touch pulled him out of his nightmare of memories. The anger and guilt released the grip they held onto his heart as he readied himself to focus on finding a killer and thus finding Nikolai.

"What have you found out? Did you speak with Jace last night?" Dac turned to face Emmaline. She nodded, and together they walked down the hall in silence, with only the sounds of their footsteps echoing off the concrete floor. Ascending the steps to the main floor and then the next, he knew she was waiting to reveal what she had learned.

171

They met with Quentin in the dining room upstairs. Quentin had already filled their glasses with deep red liquid. The three of them each took their customary places at the table. After a moment of reflection, Emmaline recounted the details of Jace's story while they sipped on their nightly blood donations. The men listened intently until she reached the end.

"This mystery person at the engagement party, it has to be her," Emmaline said when she finished her story.

"Do you think it could be Una? She fits the description with the long black hair." Quentin suggested.

Dac thought about this a moment before responding. "It's quite possible, but so does someone else."

"You can't be suggesting...." Emmaline and Quentin both said in unison.

"I don't want to think it either, but we can't rule it out. You both said she'd been acting strangely lately. Plus, I know she's been drinking from humans. That first night I came home, I saw her when she returned from her walk. She had blood stains on her mouth." Both Quentin and Emmaline gasped at this.

"I don't know. Cloe was her best friend," Emmaline replied.

"But if Dac is right, what do we tell Jace? They were good friends once too. This would devastate him, and the only thing that would do is put us all in danger." Quentin took a sip of the blood from his cup. He didn't need it, but the warm liquid calmed him.

"We don't know anything for sure yet. It's all just speculation for now. I'll go talk with my brother and find out if Una had left Noxwood at any time. Then we can decide what to do after that." Dac got up from his seat at the table, leaving Emmaline and Quentin to ponder over this realization while he went out in search of Luca.

Dac stood at the lobby entrance of Luca's apartment building. Through the window, he could see Harper pacing the room alone. He was hopeful for the chance to meet with his brother one on one, so he would wait for Luca's return. The wait would not be long, however. Luca crossed the building threshold only moments later. He laid eyes on Dac immediately. The warmth of the night only intensified with the tension felt between the two brothers.

"I haven't found your friend yet. I told you I would come to you when I have." Luca sidestepped past his brother, but Dac cut him off. "Listen, I have a deal with Harper's friend Jace. He has Nikolai hidden somewhere. That's all I know for now." Luca assured him.

"Looks like our little vampire hunter is making deals all over town. But that's not why I am here."

"Umm." Luca looked surprised to see Jace went to Dac also, but surprisingly he didn't ask what deal they made. "Then what do you want?" Luca asked.

"I need some information about Una."

"Una? Why?"

"Because she may be the one who killed our vampire hunter's fiancée? So, I need to know, had she left Noxwood at all around that time?"

"What makes you think she's the one who did? She had no reason." Luca said in defense of Una.

"Let's just say she fits the description of our vampire of interest."

"That doesn't tell me anything. I need more to go on than that."

"I had Emmaline go talk to Jace. He trusts her. He told her about an incident that happened at a party. He spotted someone who didn't seem like they belonged, but he had only seen the back of her head—someone with long black hair. Sound Familiar? Anyway, later that evening, he found Cloe alone, tired, and confused. A few weeks later, she was dead. Sounds to me like the vampire began feeding from her that night and probably a few times more after that, don't you think? And who do we know with long black hair? Una."

"I see." Luca continued walking. Dac stuck to his side, waiting for an answer. He could sense the wheels in Luca's head turning and wondered if Luca would come to the same conclusion he had while listening to Emmaline tell Jace's story. There was one other vampire with long black hair. One that had been walking around for months with a dark secret and the heaviness of guilt hanging over her head. One who wasn't Una but looked exactly like her.

"So, what do we do?" Luca finally asked.

"We do nothing. I just needed confirmation from you. I'll take care of everything." Dac left his brother alone to hunt for his nightly meal. It was time to put the beginning touches of his plan into action.

HARPER STARED OUT OF the window of the apartment. Dac was standing beside the building next to Luca. What could he have to speak about with his brother? Had Dac found Nikolai? She wished she could hear the two of them speaking, but it appeared that one of them had blocked her vampiric hearing. Whatever it was they were talking about someone didn't want her to know.

She watched as the two brothers contentiously walked away from the building. Luca was going out to feed. Harper had chosen to stay behind, only now she was beginning to regret that decision. She desperately wanted to know what Dac, and Luca were saying.

She was pacing the apartment again. She had been pacing all night, stopping only long enough to peer out the window and spot Dac approach his brother as he stepped out of the building. The curiosity was growing too much for her to handle. She shook her hands out, trying to stop the tingling in her fingertips. She walked back and forth from the living room to the kitchen. Momentarily she leaned with her elbows on the kitchen countertop, her fingernails tapping the cool granite. Then she began pacing again.

The room was starting to feel warm, and the walls felt like they were closing in around her. Blood. She needed blood, human blood, and human life. She snatched the keys off the counter and checked that her phone was still in the back pocket of the jeans she wore. Locking the door, she slammed it shut behind her and raced for the elevator.

She watched the number of each floor light up as the elevator made its slow descent to the ground floor lobby. It felt like an eternity as the hunger inside her intensified. The bell pinged as the elevator came to an abrupt stop. Harper looked up to see the doors open, not on the ground floor but another. The scent of floral perfume and human blood assaulted her as a woman entered through the elevator doors. Harper looked away, clenching her jaw and fists tightly while she tried ignoring her vampiric instincts.

The elevator came to a stop again. This time it stopped at the lobby. Harper allowed the woman to exit first, then followed behind her into the warm dark summer night.

Tonight would not be like the others since she had been hunting with Luca. Tonight, Harper needed more than a glamour and friendly pursuit. Tonight, she needed the rush of coming up on her prey unexpectantly. She wanted to feel the struggle and the fight as she sunk her teeth into her victim and stole their very life force.

She concealed herself in the darkness the way she learned by entering the mind of her victim, convincing her she was alone. The waft of the woman's perfume lingered in the warm breeze. She had walked two or three blocks away from the apartment. Harper continued following impatiently, waiting for the perfect moment to strike.

The myriad of sounds around them was grating to Harper's ears. Car horns honking and music blaring from nearby establishments. People chatting on the sidewalk. But Harper stayed focused on her prey.

She followed the woman around the corner. This street was quieter than the last. A couple holding hands walked past them. Then another group of four or five friends. And then, finally, they were alone on the street, just Harper and the woman from the elevator.

Harper lunged forward, grabbing the woman with both hands and dragging her into the nearby alleyway. The woman's purse fell to the ground, and she helplessly kicked and screamed. She flailed her arms about as she struggled to fight off her attacker. Harper giggled at the woman's fruitless attempts to free herself.

Harper turned the woman's body around so they were face to face. The woman's eyes widened as she recognized her. Harper grinned, baring her sharp fangs. She pulled the woman in close to her. Their bodies were touching—the warm skin of the human against the cold skin of the vampire. The woman continued struggling in Harper's arms. Harper held her tight in one arm while brushing the air away from her neck with the other. The vein pulsed with blood and fear. Harper sunk her teeth deep into the woman's flesh.

The woman's cries grew quieter with every ounce of blood Harper drew from her veins until finally, she was silent. Her body went limp, and Harper let her fall to the ground. Blood stained Harper's lips and the woman's neck. The scent of floral perfume lingered. The night was still.

Harper stayed in the alley for a while. The dead woman lay lifeless a few feet away from her. She listened to the sounds of the city, no longer a mélange of noise but a soft melody of liveliness and hopefulness.

Her phone buzzed in her pocket. She wanted to ignore it, but instead, she removed it from her pocket. She didn't recognize the number that lit up across the dark screen, so she pressed ignore. She twirled the phone around in her hands a few times before slipping it back into its place in the back pocket of her black jeans. Suddenly she found herself wondering about Luca again as she realized the disappointment she felt in the pit of her stomach that the call hadn't come from him. She pulled herself off the ground she'd been sitting on and gathered the dead woman's purse tossing it in the dumpster that stood in the back of the alleyway. Then she disposed of the woman's body like she had all the others and made her way home to await Luca's return.

Twenty-Six

Jace wasn't expecting an answer so quickly, but here was Dac standing in front of him at his doorstep only two days after they last spoke. He still heard no word from Alex or Luca, which made him suspicious of what they could be hiding.

Jace's hands shook at his sides. His heart beat a little quicker than normal against his chest. He had waited weeks for what he was about to hear, and he could wait no longer. He stepped aside and allowed Dac to enter his home. They stood in the kitchen, and Jace offered Dac a seat at the table, but Dac refused.

"You found Cloe's killer? Who is it?" Jace asked impatiently.

"Yes, I know who it was." Dac circled around Jace.

"Who is it?" Jace asked again. Dac raised a hand to quiet him.

"Be patient. There is something I need you to do for me."

"I'm giving you back your friend. I don't think you're in a position to be making additional demands."

Dac grabbed Jace by the throat, lifting him off his feet. His nails pierced into his skin. Jace held his breath and Dac's gaze until Dac released him. "There is more to this situation than you realize, hunter," Dac said as he placed Jace back on the ground. "I will tell you where to find your vampire, but you will follow my instructions to the T, and no more deals with other vampires. Got that."

Jace shook his head in understanding. He sat down in the chair next to him and rested his arm on the kitchen table. Then he kicked out the chair across from where he sat, insisting Dac have a seat. The vampire accepted this time and laid out his plan for Jace to follow.

179

Dac left without revealing the name or location of the vampire he says killed Cloe, though he promised Jace he would get this information in a few days' time. Jace wondered if he could trust Dac, but he still had Nikolai, and until he had what he wanted, Nikolai would stay hidden.

Jace stared out the front door after the vampire left. It was a clear night. The moon lit up the sky, and the stars twinkled in their visible constellations. The street lamps reflected off the pavement in the distance, but that's when Jace noticed the lights in front of his house were out.

A breeze came through that made Jace shiver. He stepped out onto his front porch. He looked left and then right. The streets were quiet. No cars had passed by in a while. All the neighbors were indoors. No lights shined in any windows. The only sound was the leaves blowing with the wind.

Jace went back inside, closing the door tightly behind him and locking it. He took the hawthorn branches he kept in the house and placed them around all the doors and windows. He'd had enough of visits from vampires for one night. When he was finished, he grabbed a beer from the refrigerator, lounged comfortably on his couch, and turned on his tv. It felt good to do something so ordinary and human. He just wanted a few hours of not thinking of vampires and Cloe and revenge. He wanted a few hours just to feel normal. Tomorrow he would go and talk to Sarah.

CLOE GRABBED HIS HAND and smiled as she dragged him away from his desk. His office was arranged differently than he remembered. The desk sat cattycorner to the right of the window instead of directly in front of it. There was a wood bookshelf painted black. It covered the entire left wall. But his office didn't have a bookshelf. It didn't matter. Cloe's smile was all that mattered. He followed her out of the room. Her curly hair bounced off her shoulders as she walked. He followed her outside, where the afternoon sun shone bright and warm. He looked around them. They were in a park. Cloe sat in the grass, picking at the yellow dandelions that grew from the soil. She wrapped the stem around her finger. She looked up at Jace as he stepped toward her. The hem of her dress swung in the light breeze. She raised a hand and waved to him. The smile never wavering from her face. When he reached the spot where she sat, she was gone. Jace lay down in the grass in the same place where Cloe had just been. He stared up into the sun, soaking his face in its warm rays. A blanket of happiness wrapped around him.

THE WARM RAYS OF THE sun penetrated through the glass windows heating his exposed skin. Jace rubbed his eyes as he adjusted to the morning brightness. He planted his feet on the floor while he scanned the room. Nothing seemed amiss, though he still felt uneasy. He noticed the hawthorn he had placed around the house the night before, and that's when he remembered his visit from Dac. Disappointment flooded him as he realized his score with the vampires was far from over.

He searched around the couch cushions for his phone. When he didn't find it there, he went into the kitchen and found it lying on the table. He picked it up and typed in a text to Sarah, then went into the bathroom to shower and get ready to start the day.

By the time he returned to the kitchen, Sarah had responded to his text. He grabbed his car keys and headed out the door to meet her. He decided he would grab coffee and breakfast on the way to her house.

As he neared the Aura Springs Café, he decided not to stop in. This morning he would go somewhere different. He couldn't face the café today. He couldn't face the memories that lived in that place. Instead, he stopped by a local bakery and ordered two iced coffees for himself and Sarah and a hot coffee for Brigid. He ordered a few croissants for the ladies and a buttered roll for himself which he ate in the car.

Jace grabbed the bag of croissants and the tray of coffees from his car when he arrived at Sarah's house. As he entered the house, Sarah grabbed the bag from him and placed the pastries on a plate and set them on the countertop in the kitchen. She took a bite of one and sipped her iced coffee. Sarah called out to her grandmother. Jace leaned his back against the counter. They waited for Brigid to appear before talking about the vampires and the next steps of their plan.

Brigid finally entered the kitchen. Her cane clacked against the tiled floor. Her sunglasses perched on the bridge of her nose. She took a croissant from the plate and wrapped it in a napkin, then walked to the back door and stepped outside to her favorite spot on the patio. Sarah and Jace followed behind her, Sarah carrying the coffees.

Outside, the trees that lined Sarah's backyard provided shade from the hot late morning sun. Birds chirped as they flew by. Two squirrels ran around the yard, playfully climbing up and down the trees. Jace sat and absorbed all the beauty of this summer morning before beginning talks about the grim nights ahead.

"Dac came to see me at my house last night," Jace said, "he says he knows who killed Cloe, but he wants me to do something for him before he tells me who it is." He continued with the details of Dac's plan as he had laid them out the night before.

"And he wants all this to go down within the next two days?" Sarah asked.

"Yup. And he says I should be expecting a visit from Luca tonight. Afterward, I should contact Alex. I should arrange a meeting place which Dac has given to me. Two nights from tonight, Dac will reveal the true location of Cloe's killer. I am to set Nikolai free. Dac and Luca will be at the meeting place to take care of Alex, and we are to do what we will with the one vampire that killed Cloe."

"And that's it? He is just going to allow us to kill a vampire with no repercussions?" Sarah asked.

"That's what he said, so long as we don't go after any other vampires. He says they will leave us alone if we leave them alone."

"I don't know, sounds suspicious," Brigid said. "I've dealt with Dac in the past when I was hunting vampires. I think there's more to it than what he's saying."

"Even if it is, what other choice do we have other than to go along with it?" Jace took a sip of his iced coffee, stirring the ice around with his straw.

"Just be careful. Come to me before you head over to wherever he sends you. You'll need a plan in case it's a trap." Brigid finished the last bite of her croissant and took the last sip of her coffee before grabbing her cane.

"We will," Sarah said to her grandmother before Brigid entered through the door to go back inside the house. Jace and Sarah remained on the back patio for a while, talking about anything and everything else that had nothing to do with vampires.

Light grey clouds began rolling in by midafternoon, producing a gentle summer rain. The squirrels that had been playing in the yard had retreated to the shelter of the leafy branches of one of the many trees in Sarah's yard. The air took on an earthy smell as the raindrops moistened the once dry land. Sarah and Jace returned to the shelter of Sarah's living room. They ordered food for dinner to be delivered and casually enjoyed each other's company while they waited.

It was already dark by the time Jace had left Sarah's house. He wanted to be at his own house when Luca came to see him. He promised Sarah and her grandmother he would return first thing the next morning.

The entire drive home Jace contemplated Dac's plan. There was one part he had to admit that didn't make sense. What was he supposed to tell Alex why he was giving up Nikolai and Dac without Alex holding up his end of their bargain? It didn't matter, though, because as he pulled into his driveway, he found Alex waiting by his front door.

The vampire was at Jace's car door before he even had time to cut off the engine. Jace placed the car in park and dimmed the headlights though he kept the car running for what reason he wasn't sure. He opened the car door and stepped out of the driver's seat. His palms were sweating, and he wiped them against his pants.

Alex handed him a piece of paper. It was difficult to read the writing in the dark, but he could tell it contained only one word, possibly a name. He took his cell phone out of his pocket and used the light on the screen to read the note.

"What is this?" He asked the vampire.

"The answer you've been looking for. Now it's your turn. Where are Nikolai and Dac?" Alex demanded.

Jace swallowed hard. He wasn't prepared for this encounter. "Where did you get this?" he asked, trying to buy a little time to think of a response.

Alex grabbed him by the throat, slamming his back up against the car so hard Jace heard his window crack. "I held up my end. I got you what you wanted. Now you will get me what I want," Alex growled.

"How did you get this," Jace demanded one more time. "How do I know this is true."

"From your old friend Quentin. Does that satisfy you enough?" Alex was still holding onto Jace's throat, though he had loosened his grip some.

It started to make sense now. This was part of Dac's plan. "I'll arrange for everything the day after tomorrow. I'll have an address for you then."

"Fine." Alex let go of Jace and turned as though he was going to leave, and then he turned back. "But you better have them by then. Otherwise, I'll be back for you. And next time, I won't be so nice."

SCORNED IN DARKNESS

Alex was gone in a flash. Jace looked around at the empty neighborhood. The street was still wet from the rain earlier that day that had lasted well into the evening. He examined his broken window. That was going to cost him. He leaned into his car, careful not to get cut by the broken glass. He turned off the engine and removed his keys, then wandered into the house, looking at the name on the paper, while he awaited his next visitor.

Twenty-Seven

Emmaline was at the apartment talking to Luca. She asked to speak with him privately, so Harper went out for a walk. Instead, she found herself on the building rooftop. The daytime had produced a rain that lasted well into the evening hours, leaving the surfaces sprinkled with lingering raindrops and the air smelling like fresh earth. She wiped the ledge with her hand and sat with her feet dangling over the edge as she looked down into the dark city illuminated with its artificial lights giving its people a false sense of safety.

She watched the many humans hurry to their destinations, unaware of the monster lurking above them. She used to be one of those humans. Carefree and blissfully ignorant. She envied them now.

On the ground of the rooftop, shards of broken glass glistened like the night stars that sparkled in the sky. She picked one up and studied it in her hands. The edges were sharp. She touched her fingertip to the most pointed edge, pressing until the skin broke. She held her hand out over the empty sky and watched the blood trickle out of her fingertip and drip out into the crowd below.

Someone from the street down below her looked up towards the rooftop. She could sense their curiosity and concern, and she flashed her pearly white fanged smile down at them as if to dare them to come and save her even though she knew they could not see her from that far distance. Or could they?

Moments later, she heard the door open that accessed the roof from inside the building. Standing there was a young man. On his forehead was her smeared blood that he had tried to wipe away when it had fallen from the sky and dripped onto him. What could be more perfect than her meal coming to her tonight? She almost pitied the man. There he was, the good Samaritan, thinking he was doing his good deed for the day. He was going to save the girl from harming herself further and jumping off the rooftop. His innocence radiated out of his pores. His blood smelled sweet like sugar.

Harper gently swung her feet back around the ledge and planted them on the ground underneath her. The young man smiled and reached out his hand to her. "It's ok," he said.

"Is it?" Harper asked.

"Yes," he replied, stepping slowly towards her. "Whatever it is, I'm sure there's a solution. Just give me your hand. Let me help you." He was still holding out his hand. When he was close enough, Harper reached out and grabbed his hand, gently wrapping it in hers. She stood up from the ledge so that she was standing eye to eye with the young man still holding his hand.

"That's it," the man said as he pulled her closer to him to lead her away from the edge. "Your hand is so cold. Are you sick?" He asked.

"Yes," Harper replied. "I'm sick. A blood disease." She winked as she said it.

"Is that why you're up here? Is there treatment?" he continued his questioning with genuine concern and curiosity.

"Treatment. Yes, there is a treatment. I just need new blood." Harper smiled crookedly and flashed her fangs watching the man's eyes widened as he realized the true nightmare he had walked into on top of this building. He had thought he was saving the life of a fragile girl when in fact, he had stepped into the clutches of a vile creature.

She tightened her grip on his hand and grasped the back of his neck with her other hand. Before the man had time to put up a fight, she sunk her teeth into the side of his throat. She drank until his body fell limp, then she tossed him over the building's edge

Harper exited the rooftop and rode the elevator back to the 13th floor. She opened the door to Luca's apartment. Emmaline was gone, and Luca was sitting on the couch, his right leg crossed over the left. No matter how long she stayed there, this still hadn't felt like home. And no matter how close she and Luca became, she still felt like an intruder.

She was once his prisoner, although it turned out Alex was the true mastermind behind her kidnapping. But now, she was the one who went to him for help, and he was kind enough to help her. He helped Jace, a human he would have normally fed off. He taught her how to hunt properly and showed her she didn't have to feel guilty for being herself. But somehow, he was still a stranger in her eyes.

"Hey," Luca looked her way when he heard her enter the room.

"Hi," she said shyly, not really sure why she felt so insecure.

"I see you've fed."

"Yea."

"Good. I need to go. And I need you to stay here. My brother is up to something. I'm not exactly sure what it is, but I promise I will keep you safe."

"You think I'm still in danger from him? What is going on?" Harper asked. "Why was Emmaline here, and what were you and Dac talking about out on the sidewalk last night?" The questions stumbled out her mouth one after the other.

"He thinks he knows who killed your old friend Cloe."

"Oh. He does?" She began fidgeting the way she did whenever someone mentioned Cloe's death. "Who does he think it was?"

"Una." Luca was a matter of fact in his answer.

"Oh my God. Do you think he's right?"

"It's possible, I guess." He didn't sound convinced, but for a moment, Harper felt her heart rate calm down a beat.

"Then why do you think I'm still in danger from him?"

"Because you helped free your friend Jace, who still has Nikolai hidden somewhere captive. He blames you for that, and you and I both know Dac isn't the forgiving type. Now promise me you'll stay here. I won't be long."

Harper nodded, and Luca left out the door. Once again, she found herself nervously pacing the apartment. The fresh human blood inside her began to run cold. Her skin itched. She went to the kitchen and began opening all the drawers. They were all empty. She looked inside the closets, but only plastic hangers hung with freshly washed clothes. Frantically she searched the articles of clothing. She checked inside the pockets and scanned the surfaces. She found nothing. Slamming the closet door shut, she moved on into the bathroom. She stood in the doorway staring across at the mirror above the bathroom sink, glaring at her repulsive reflection. Slowly she stepped forward. She raised her fist above her shoulder. Swinging forward, she smashed the mirror.

The glass shattered around her. She stood and watched as the pieces fell into the sink and onto the floor. She picked up a large piece of the broken glass and held it in front of her face. She grabbed another—a smaller piece, its edge pointy and sharp. Still staring into the larger glass, she brought the smaller piece to her cheek and sliced it across her face.

IT WAS NEARING MORNING when Jace heard the faint knock on his door. He was halfway between sleep and awake. The pounding on the door grew louder. He groggily moved off of the couch he had fallen asleep on and walked across the room to answer the door. The color of the dark midnight sky was already changing to a lighter blue. The sun was not yet rising, but it soon would be. Luca stood outside Jace's house. His silhouette illuminated by the yellow porch light. Jace moved to the side, allowing Luca to step inside.

"I don't have much time, as you can see," Luca said to him. "Here," He pushed a folded piece of paper into Jace's hand. "I believe this is what you're looking for."

Jace unfolded the paper. He rubbed his eyes as he read the name scribbled in ink. "Why not just tell me?" he asked, thinking of how Alex had also given him a note. It seemed a little archaic to him.

"It's safer this way," Was all Luca said about it. "Now, about Alex..."

"I'll set up a meeting for tomorrow and send you the details later tonight," Jace interrupted. "You should go before the sun comes up." Luca nodded and was gone so fast that Jace barely noticed him leave.

Jace looked down at the note in his hand one more time. He took the note he had gotten from Alex earlier and compared the two. Both had the same name. He had been unsure if Alex was being truthful, but now he was more inclined to believe he had the correct name. Still, he was unsure exactly what Dac was planning, though he had to agree with Brigid. Dac was definitely up to something more. Otherwise, he could have given Jace the information on his own. He could have had his friend back sooner, but instead, he sent Luca and Alex with the same information, clearly each of them expecting Jace to hold up his end to the bargains he had made. It didn't matter much to him what Dac planned to do with these two. He had what he needed. In a few hours, he would head back over to Sarah's, and he, Sarah, and Brigid would decide their next steps to finding the vampire whose name was on this paper. In the meantime, Jace would get a few extra hours of sleep.

His alarm went off precisely at 9 o'clock that morning. He hit the snooze button a total of three times before finally rolling himself out of bed and into the shower. He didn't even bother making coffee before he headed out to Sarah's house.

When he reached Sarah's, she and Brigid were already on the back patio. As he made his way around to the back of the house, he could smell the mixing scents of grass, bacon, and coffee. His stomach started to rumble, and he remembered he had not had anything to eat since some time the night before.

Sarah offered him some of the bacon, toast, and fresh fruit they had set out on the table. He gladly accepted, putting some of each onto a plate and then taking his usual seat. He handed Sarah the two sheets of paper with the name of the vampire and explained each of the visits he'd had the night before and earlier that morning.

Brigid grabbed her cane and began walking into the house. She turned to Sarah and asked her to talk inside but requested that Jace stay outside so they could speak privately. Jace sat back in his chair and continued eating while the two women went inside to talk. Sarah closed the door behind her, and Jace wished he could hear what they were talking about beyond the glass door. It reminded him of the other day when he had come over and overheard them talking in the kitchen. He knew that Brigid didn't trust him completely. He wished she did. No matter what she thought, he was ready to take on the vampires.

Thirty minutes later, Sarah came back outside. Jace was still seated in the same chair, looking through his phone, wiping the sweat from his forehead. He pretended not to notice her. Not that he was mad, he was just worried she felt the same way as her grandmother.

"Hey," Sarah said when she sat down next to Jace.

"Hey," Jace barely looked up except to reach for the pitcher of ice water on the table. The ice had mostly melted, and condensation was running down the sides of the glass. He poured the water into an empty cup. When he took a sip, the water was nearly warm from the heated temperature outside. Still, it was mildly refreshing.

"I know what you're thinking," Sarah said.

"Do you?" Jace barely looked at her, only glancing in her direction.

"It's not that she doesn't trust you. She's just not sure you have the stomach for it. You're a good guy, Jace." Sarah rested a hand on Jace's knee in an attempt to reassure him.

"Oh, and she believes you have the stomach for it. Are you not a good person then?" Jace tried to hold back the sarcasm, but it spilled out of him with contempt.

"It's different for me. I was born for this. It's in my blood." Sarah removed her hand from his knee as she defended her grandmother's concerns.

"That may be, but they killed my fiancée. I will get justice for her, no matter what I have to do. I'm ready for this." Jace took another drink of water, then got up from his seat and walked to the edge of the patio, looking out over the yard.

"I believe you," Sarah said. She stood behind him and put her hand on his shoulder.

"So, what's next?" Jace looked over his shoulder at Sarah. "We still need to know where this vampire is. For now, all I have is a name."

"We wait and see what Dac says tonight. You did say he was supposed to contact you, right?"

"Yes, he said he would," Jace assured her. "I'll demand the location of the vampire before I release Nikolai."

"And if he doesn't give it. Don't worry, we'll find her. We still have the music box." Sarah reminded him.

Jace turned to face Sarah, knowing she was correct. No matter what happened later on with Dac, they still had the music box. They still had a way to find the vampire. And they would.

Twenty-Eight

It was midnight when Dac finally contacted Jace with the rest of the plan. He didn't show up at his house this time but had called him over the phone. "You will know her when you see her. You have seen her once before," is what Dac had said to him about the vampire. He had given Jace two addresses which Jace had jotted down on a slice of paper. One of the addresses he was to provide to both Alex and Luca, instructing them to arrive there at different times. The other address would be the place he could find the vampire he had been seeking this whole time—the vampire who had caused Cloe's death. Dac confessed to giving Alex and Luca a fake name to hand over to him. "You will understand why I had to do that when the time comes," Dac had said. "As I've said before, do what you will with her, then leave the rest of us alone, and we will do the same with you." The line was silent for a moment.

"For reassurance, where have you been keeping Nikolai?" Dac finally asked Jace.

"In the morgue."

"Very clever," and then, before disconnecting the call, Dac said, "free Nikolai tomorrow night and give his location to Luca. Have him and Harper meet you there."

Jace stared at the blank screen on his phone, contemplating who to talk to first, Alex or Luca. He decided on Alex. Alex was the more unstable one. Jace knew he was waiting impatiently. It wouldn't be long before Alex grew restless again. So, he reached out, and within minutes Alex was at his doorstep.

Jace handed Alex a strip of paper with the address written down. "Arrive there alone tomorrow," Jace told him.

"Why tomorrow?" Alex demanded. "Why not tonight?"

"Tomorrow was the earliest I could arrange for the transport of both bodies," Jace replied.

"So, you have both of them now?"

"Yes, just as agreed upon."

"Fine then, I will see you tomorrow. Hopefully, for the last time." Alex shoved the strip of paper in his pocket and was gone.

Jace breathed out a sigh of relief and readied himself for his next encounter. Luca, at least, was more patient and much less hostile. Same as Alex, he didn't want to discuss anything over a phone call or text. He wanted the information written on paper and handed to him. He said it was the best way of keeping this information safe. He wouldn't even read it until the very last minute, worried somehow Alex would find a way to extract the thoughts from his mind and elude their plan.

Jace placed two sheets of paper inside an envelope. One with the address of where Alex would be and the other with the address of Nikolai's location. When Luca arrived at his doorstep, Jace handed him the envelope. Luca said nothing as he took it from Jace's hands. He nodded once and then vanished into the dark cover of night.

Inside of the house was suddenly dark and quiet. Jace reached for the light switch when something grabbed him by the throat. Her pale skin glowed in contrast to the dark room, and her bright white fanged teeth sparkled as she sneered at him. "Take me to Nikolai now, and I won't kill you," The voice demanded before loosening her grip.

Jace recognized the voice as Una. "He's dead. I'm handing him over to Alex tomorrow," he lied while rubbing the side of his neck.

"You and I both know that isn't true, and I need him tonight." She insisted.

Jace tried to move away from her, but she blocked his way. Knowing it was useless to keep trying to evade her, he said, "Look, I already made a deal with your son, and I'm a man of my word."

"You are a man of many words. Now for the last time, take me to Nikolai, NOW!" She hissed at him.

"I told you, I already promised him to Alex. I made the arrangements for tomorrow evening. There's no way I can get him tonight."

"You can and you will," she insisted one more time. "For the sake of my son, we need to get him tonight. And besides, you'll be needing all of tomorrow's daylight hours if you're planning on killing your vampire tomorrow night."

"What are you talking about?"

"I'm well aware of your plans and all the deals you've been making with vampires lately. I told you that night in the church I won't let any harm come to my son. Now, let's go." She grabbed Jace by the arm and dragged him outside to his parked car. She reached through his broken window, unlocked the door to open it, and pushed him inside.

Jace fished the keys out of his pocket and fumbled to put them in the ignition. Una was in the passenger seat next to him before he could get the car started. He carefully pulled out of the driveway and drove towards the morgue where he had been hiding Nikolai. The night's warm breeze blew in through the broken window. The whole drive over, he had been searching for ideas to get inside. Without his contact at the morgue, he had no idea how he was going to retrieve Nikolai's body.

He parked his car as close to the building as he could in hopes that no one passing by would notice it. Both he and Una stepped out of the car. The gravel on the pavement crunched under his feet. Una walked silently beside him. When they reached the door to the morgue, he turned to her. "He's in here, but I don't know how we're supposed to get inside."

Una gently pushed Jace aside. She wrapped her hand around the door handle. Pulling on it with all her vampiric strength, she yanked the metal door open and stepped inside. Jace stared at her, amazed at the strength and grace with which she used to open the door. He knew vampires were strong but had never truly witnessed such force as this. She glared at him from over her shoulder, "you coming?" She asked. Jace shrugged and entered through the doorway, knowing he did not have much choice.

They walked through the dark hallway. Jace struggled to see, but Una was clearly not having that same issue. Of course, she wouldn't. She was a vampire. They were made to see in the dark.

"Where is he? Can we hurry this up, please?" Una demanded of him.

"I don't know exactly," Jace said. "All these doors look the same in the dark. Besides, I've never been in here on my own."

"Well, you better figure it out," She made a motion as if she were sniffing the air. "I can't sense him here." She said.

"Because he's frozen. That was the point of putting him here."

"Frozen?" Una stopped in her tracks.

"Don't worry. I was assured he'd be just fine. We just have to find him and thaw him out." Jace continued looking for something familiar in the dark halls. The irritation and impatience that radiated off of Una let him know he needed to find the room where Nikolai was being kept sooner rather than later.

The green double doors at the end of the hall came into view, and Jace felt a twinge of relief as a sense of familiarity rushed over him. The room he was looking for was just beyond those doors. He picked up his pace, with his vampire companion keeping close at his side.

When they finally reached the room that housed Nikolai, of course, the door was locked. Una again used her vampiric strength to open the door with an ease Jace could only imagine. Inside the room, the air was cold, damp, and smelled of death.

"Where is he?" Una demanded, looking at the wall of steel drawers.

"The bottom one, down there," Jace said, pointing to the corner drawer.

Una grasped the handle and yanked the draw open. A rush of cold and icy steam came rushing out. Using her sharp fingernails, she cut through the tape holding together the cardboards pieces that surrounded him and quickly began to unwrap him. She gasped at the sight of Nikolai's ice-cold body laid out on the cool metal slab. His dark hair and eyebrows covered in bits of icy frost.

She grabbed a lab coat that had been hanging on a hook nearby and wrapped it around Nikolai in an attempt to warm him. She wiped his hair dry as the frost began to melt. Una hissed at Jace when he tried to come near them to help out. He found her sudden protectiveness over Nikolai quite remarkable, considering it was only a few short months ago that she had tried to kill him. But he kept this thought to himself.

Jace found a stool in the other corner of the room and took a seat. The room remained dark, with only a touch of light from the outside peaking in through the tiny windows. He watched as Una bit into her wrist and rubbed her blood against Nikolai's lips. Nikolai moaned as he came to life and grasped onto Una's wrist, drinking in the blood from her vein. Jace turned his head away, ashamed of witnessing such an intimate yet horrific moment in this stark reminder of the creatures the vampires really were.

Once Nikolai recovered enough of his strength, he and Una walked out together as if Jace was not even there. Jace sat alone in the dark room of the morgue. Suddenly all too aware of all the dead bodies possibly keeping him company in this room, he hurried out down the hall in which he came and exited the building.

Sitting in his car, still parked in the darkest part of the parking lot closest to the building, Jace thought about what had just happened and what he had just done. He basically just delivered Nikolai to the one who had recently tried to kill him and who had almost succeeded.

He banged his fist against the steering wheel. "Shit! Shit! Shit!" He screamed at no one. What if Una kills him now? What will Dac do if Nikolai doesn't show up tomorrow? What had he just done? But he hadn't had much choice. Una would have killed him if he hadn't done what she asked.

Jace jumped out of the car. Standing in the pitch-dark parking lot, he searched the area around him. But he knew it was useless. There was no trace of Una or Nikolai. Vampires were much faster than humans. They were, of course, long gone by now. There was only one thing left for Jace to do.

When he arrived back at his house, he quickly went inside and gathered a few essential things for the next day's trip. Inside his duffle bag, he stuffed a change of clothes along with the creams and oils that Brigid had given him to protect himself against the vampires. Lastly, he pulled the leather case from atop his closet shelf. From it, he unsheathed the blade that it kept protected. He glared down at the dagger he now held in his hand. The leather-wrapped handle was warm against his skin. Harper had given it to him for protection. He wondered whether she knew what he intended to do with it now. He replaced the blade back into its leather casing and dropped it into the duffle bag. Next, he texted Sarah to let her know he was on the way to her house tonight.

On the drive over to Sarah's, he kept the music playing loud in his car. The roads were dark with dimmed streetlights. He used the high beams to brighten up the way. Shadows bounced off the asphalt in front of him. His mind raced with thoughts of how the night's events had deviated from their original plans. But Una was right about one thing. If he were going to get to the address Dac had given to him before sunset, he would need all the daylight hours to get there.

Sarah was waiting for him outside of her house when he got there. She was sitting on the porch swing that hung in front of her house. The light that hung over her front door was turned on, illuminating her face as she swung back and forth in and out of the shadows. Jace parked his car in the driveway behind Sarah's. He grabbed the duffle bag from the seat next to him and swung it over his shoulder as he stepped out of the car.

"I spoke with my grandmother already. I'll fill you in on the plan once we get inside." Sarah said as Jace approached her. She stopped swinging and met Jace by the front door. As they stepped into the house, she turned to him and said, "I hope you're ready."

"I'm ready," Jace assured her. He took one last look around. Once he felt comfortable, they were alone, that no supernatural creatures were watching them, he went inside the house and secured the door behind him. The night remained quiet while they awaited the morning sunrise.

Twenty-Nine

Deciding to use the last remaining hours before sunrise to rest, Sarah went to her room, and Jace remained on the couch in Sarah's living room. He kicked off his shoes and laid back against the soft cushions. The pale blue light of the early morning sky was peeking through the blinds. Jace closed his eyes and fell into a dreamless sleep.

By the time Jace awoke, it was already mid-morning. The heat of the summer sun could be felt through the window. Sarah and her grandmother were talking in hushed voices in the kitchen. Jace picked up his duffle bag from the floor and carried it with him into the bathroom to wash up and then afterward joined Sarah and Brigid.

"We should be going," Jace said as Sarah handed him a clear plastic thermos filled with a thick green liquid inside. Jace looked quizzically at the green substance.

"It's a protein smoothie," Sarah informed him.

"You'll need to keep your energy high and your stomachs light," Brigid chimed in. "Today's the day," she said. "Good luck."

Jace adjusted the strap of his duffle bag over his shoulder. He and Sarah walked outside where they decided they would use Sarah's car due to Jace's broken window although Jace would still drive. The warm air mixed with his anxiety made Jace's stomach turn. Sarah tossed him her keys. He put their bags down in the back seat and took a drink of the smoothie. He grimaced at the slightly bitter taste. Securing the top back on the thermos, he placed it in the cupholder when he got in the car. Sarah fastened her seatbelt, and Jace drove off towards the highway.

The scenery of green shrubs and tall trees passed by in a blur as Jace sped down the road. The GPS was mostly silent once they had reached the main highway, as it would mostly be a straight drive towards their destination. Sarah turned on the radio to help fill the silence between them. He heard the crinkle of foil as Sarah unwrapped one of the energy bars her grandmother had packed for them. His stomach rumbled, and he took another drink of the smoothie.

It was early evening when they finally stopped at the rest area. Jace unscrewed the cap of the gas tank. He removed the nozzle from the pump and refilled the gas in the car. People walked through the parking lot. Families driving to and from their summer vacations stopped for food and to stretch their legs. All of them building fond memories of time spent together, laughing, and joking, and enjoying the warm summer air. Jace turned towards Sarah, who was still seated in the passenger seat, and tapped on the window. She rolled the window down and looked up at him standing over her. He had one arm leaning on the car while his other hand still held on to the gas pump. The sun was still high in the evening sky, casting specks of yellow in her eyes. With his head, he gestured towards the brick building standing in the middle of the parking lot.

"Should we see about getting a bite to eat?" He asked.

"I suppose a small bite couldn't hurt," she said.

Jace returned the gas pump, and he and Sarah walked over to the large building of the rest area. Inside was a visiting center, public restrooms, and a food court with several fast-food options. Jace ordered a burger, a side of fries, and a soda. Sarah bought herself a sandwich, a small bag of chips, and a bottled water. They sat at one of the small plastic tables and ate their food. The chatter of the many people visiting the rest stop filled the entire room. The mixed smells of grease, fried food, and cleaning chemicals turned Jace's stomach even as he stuffed his face with the food from his tray. His shoulders felt heavy and weighed down by tension. He glanced across the table at Sarah and wondered how she appeared so calm. Jace excused himself for the restroom, and Sarah did the same. Who knew when the next opportunity would arrive? They had a long trip and a long night still ahead of them. They agreed to meet back at the car and went their separate ways.

Jace stared at the clear, cool water as it ran out of the small chrome faucet rinsing the soap from his hands. The door hinges squealed as the door swung open and closed, with others entering and exiting the restroom. Sneakers squeaked across the tiled floor. Someone cleared their throat behind him, and Jace realized he must have been standing there a while too long. He splashed a small amount of water over his face. Then dried his hands and rubbed his tense shoulders as he walked out of the restroom.

When he returned to the car, Sarah was already waiting for him. Jace looked to the GPS, which said they had two more hours until they reached their destination. Jace looked at the clock on his dashboard. Two more hours until sunset. They should arrive right around the time the vampire was rising from her daytime sleep. With any luck, they would reach her before she awoke, but he knew they would be cutting it close. He sucked in a breath and drove off.

They spent the remainder of the drive discussing their plan for when they arrived. Sarah wanted to make sure Jace was still on board with their decision, that he knew what he needed to do. He humored her, but the constant second-guessing he received from her and Brigid grated on his nerves a little bit. He reassured her one last time he was ready and capable despite the constant unease stationed in the pit of his stomach. He then turned the music up until they were close to the address Dac had given him.

The GPS said three more miles until they reached their destination. Jace lowered the music and paid close attention to the voice on the GSP system. When it said turn left, he turned left. If told to make a right, he a made a right. This area was mountainous and looked slightly familiar.

The last time he had been here, it was winter and icy and cold. Now it was bursting with full leafy trees and the sounds and colors of summer.

They finally arrived. Jace's stomach turned as he parked the car a few feet away from the house. He and Sara grabbed their bags from the back seat. Jace opened his bag and removed the oils he had packed. He placed a few vials in his pocket and hung one around his neck that attached to a leather cord. Sarah did the same. The sun was just beginning to set. Colors of red and orange lined the horizon as the sun was making its inevitable descent. Jace removed the dagger from his bag. He unsheathed it from its leather covering. The orange sun rays that peaked through the plentiful trees reflected off the steel blade. Jace took the vial of oil from the bag, removed the cap, poured the oil onto a cloth, and wiped it across the blade. He then placed the dagger back in its case and hung it from the belt around his waist. He looked over at Sarah. She had a look of determination on her face and an ax in her hand. She asked one more time, "are you ready?" He nodded to her, and she nodded back. Together they walked to the house of the vampire.

The house reminded Jace of something out of the renaissance, like some kind of 16th-century French chateau, although somewhat modernized. Admittedly, had it not been for the dark shadows cast by the long-overgrown branches of surrounding trees and the threat of a vampire lurking on the inside, it would have been a beautiful place.

A tall iron gate surrounded the house like a fortress. It did not surprise Jace to find the gate was locked. He crept around the sides of the property, looking for any way inside. He heard the sound of clicking and scraping metal and looked to see Sarah at the front of the gate. She had a thin metal-type instrument in her hand, and she was working it inside the lock. He smiled at her as she pushed the gate open and followed her inside.

They stepped lightly across the stoned driveway, careful to make as little noise as possible. Jace noted the ivy vines climbing up the tiered water fountain and the neglected landscaping. A mix of brown, dead grass and overgrown weeds littered the lawn. More weeds were sprouting in between the stones of the driveway under their feet.

By the time they reached the front door, the sun was just barely peeking above the horizon. The sky was now a deep shade of dark blue, and the moon was already visible. The thick forest surrounding them made everything frighteningly darker. Sarah worked on picking the lock here, too, while Jace held out his phone to provide her a little extra light. The door creaked when she opened it. They instinctively clasped hands as they stepped into the house. Inside was almost pitch dark, with long heavy curtains covering every window, reminding Jace of the other vampire house. "She'll be awaking soon if she hasn't already," Sarah whispered. "Stay aware and be careful." Jace nodded and gently squeezed her hand. Knowing they would have little time before the vampire would retain her full strength, they split up in search of her hiding place.

Sarah took the upstairs, and Jace searched the lower level. After spending time with the vampires last winter and remembering how they kept their rooms underground, he surmised it would be the same here, and he prayed he was correct. He wanted to get to the vampire before Sarah. He wanted to strike the first blow. He wanted to be the one to kill this vampire. No matter what happened, he was going to get justice for Cloe. He deserved that. She deserved that.

Cold, damp, stone steps led down to the lowest level of the house. Jace held on to the wall with one hand, using it as a guide as he descended down the dank stairwell. He calculated each step as he navigated his way around in the dark, not wanting to alert the vampire too early of his presence. Finally, he reached what appeared to be a doorway. He clutched the knife that hung on his side. With his free hand, he took his phone from his pocket and, using the light of the screen, he surveyed the room as best he could. It seemed to be an open room. He saw no coffins, no bed, or any other type of furniture. Determining there was no vampire sleeping in here, he turned to walk away until the glimmer of something on the far wall caught his eye. He could not see much with only the back screen light of his phone, but he noticed a small lantern hanging on the wall. He turned it on. The light was faint, but it was enough for him to see and what he saw shocked him.

Metal chains hung from the far wall. Pieces of broken glass were scattered everywhere. Blood stained the floor. Emmaline's tale of what happened to Harper and Nikolai just a few months earlier came flooding into his memory. Suddenly he realized where he was. He was standing in the room where Harper had been held captive by Alex. The same room where Una had stabbed Nikolai. This was Luca's house.

Jace turned to leave the room. He raced up the stairs to find Sarah. As he reached the top and found himself back on the main level of the house, he noticed a light on in the room next to the foyer. His stomach turned to knots. His palms began to sweat. His heart beat hard in his chest. The vampire appeared in the doorway. Her thick blonde locks cascaded past her shoulders. She made no attempt to hide her fangs as she smiled at the sight of him.

"Well, it's not every day my dinner comes to me." She said playfully. Jace noticed her graceful steps as she moved closer to him. A haze fell over him, and he tried to break free from the vampire's gaze, but she held him in her vampiric trance. He wrestled with the hold she was taking on his mind. He remembered Brigid once saying to keep the mind sharp and think of anything and everything to distract his thoughts away from the vampire. He had to keep the vampire out of his head. He started thinking of Cloe and using those memories to keep him reminded of why he was here. He thought about the engagement party and the mystery woman with the long dark hair. Then memories of last winter and the poker games in the warehouse started rushing to the forefront. Zaine sitting next to him at the table, the glass shattering behind the bar, the card dealer, the shadow of a woman at the back of the room, they were all connected. The bartender was Alex. The card dealer was standing in front of him now. Could that unknown woman have been Una? Una had long black hair like Harper's. Could Dac have sent him to Una? But that was not the name Alex or Luca had given him. Dac had said he had given them the wrong name. He said Jace would soon understand. He finally felt his mind breaking free of the vampire's hold. His thoughts were becoming clear again.

"What's your name?" He asked, trying to distract her and also wanting to know if her name would match that which Dac gave to Alex and Luca. But she did not answer. Instead, she became angry. She rushed at him. Before he could grab the dagger or one of the oils, she had him by the throat. She grabbed at the leather cord around his neck, ripping it free. It went crashing to the ground. The oil inside spilled onto the floor. She pulled him closer to her.

"A hunter, though not a very good one, I see. It's been a while since I've run into one of you." She licked her lips before opening her mouth and baring her fangs. She tilted her head to the side but then stopped. "I remember you," she said, still holding tightly to his throat.

Jace choked on the saliva in his mouth. He searched his brain for a response, but words seemed elusive as he struggled for oxygen. A scream came from somewhere behind them. The vampire turned towards the sound, tossing Jace across the room. He hit his shoulder against the leg of the sofa when he landed. At the other end of the room was the entryway to what appeared to be a dining room. Jace could see the legs of a long table and chairs. He struggled to get to his feet. The blonde vampire was kneeling on the floor, holding the body of another. Jace noticed the blood flowing from the deep neck wound. The head was nearly decapitated, a head full of dark hair. Sarah stood nearby, covered in blood, ax in hand, ready to strike another blow. The blonde vampire looked up at her. Anger and hatred radiated from her as she sneered and hissed. Jace knew that feeling all too well.

She dropped the body of the dead vampire and lunged at Sarah. Jace was already on his feet. The dagger clutched in his hands. He thrust the blade into her back just as she went to bite Sarah's throat. She arched backward as she screeched in pain. Jace pulled the knife from her flesh. He stepped to the side as Sarah reached for her ax. With one swift swing, she made contact. It was over. They thought for one second.

"That's not her," Jace said as he looked at the lifeless dark-haired vampire. Her hair was covered in so much blood, and Jace had not noticed in the commotion that even though it was dark, it was not black or even a dark brown. It was a dark red, almost like Sarah's. This was not her. She was not the vampire he wanted.

Thirty

The last time Luca came home to the apartment in Aura City, he found Harper on the floor of the bathroom, surrounded by broken glass. The cuts had healed by the time he found her, but he knew what she had done, and she knew that he knew. He hadn't said anything. He just sat on the floor beside her. He cradled her in his arms, and they stayed there until the final remaining dark hour of the morning when they had to retreat to their hiding place.

This night, however, Harper watched as Luca paced the room as she had done many times over the past nights. They had gone out early to hunt, to feed. In those hours, he tried to play it cool as though it were any regular night, but Harper could sense an uneasiness in him. She asked him about it a few times, but his answer was always the same, "I'm fine. Everything is going to be fine," he would say. She knew he was not fine; nothing was fine, and she wondered if it had to do with Dac and wherever he had gone the night before.

He must have noticed her watching him because he stopped pacing. He stood in front of her, where she was seated on the couch. He reached for her hands. She placed both her hands in his. "Let's go to the roof," he said. "I want to look at the stars."

Harper rose to her feet and allowed him to lead her up to the roof. She tried not to think of the last time she stood up there. She was alone then until she wasn't when that human had come to the roof, but she didn't want to think about that now. For now, she wanted to be there for Luca, as he had in the past few weeks been there for her.

He walked to the edge of the building and stood upon the ledge. She followed. She stood next to him. Gently she grabbed his hand again. He looked over at her, and she at him. A glimmer of red flickered in his eyes. She had noticed his eyes only turned red during times of intense emotion, such as anger, and at that moment, she realized how much he must have been holding back.

"You can talk to me, you know; whatever it is, you can tell me. Maybe I can help." she had said.

"I'd rather you'd stay safe," he told her, and she knew now this was definitely about Dac.

"I'm sorry I dragged you into this." Her guilt was palpable.

"You didn't. This is my fault. My loyalty to Alex started this. I should have stopped him long ago, and I shouldn't have involved your friend Jace." Luca tried to reassure her. She could tell she was not doing a very good job at making him feel better.

"Well, if we are going to be passing blame around, then Dac is truly the one to blame here. He is the one who tried to kill you first." Harper tried to help him justify his actions.

"After I turned him into a vampire." Luca stepped off the ledge and began pacing the rooftop. "Look, I made a lot of mistakes in the beginning. There were a lot of things I could have, I should have, handled differently. But..." he faced her this time, placing his finger under her chin just as he had done the first night they had met at his house in Noxwood. His eyes once again flickered with red, and he said, "it all ends tonight."

THE BUILDING WAS SMALL, its exterior walls torn and tattered. An abandoned old hold house centered on the border of Aura Springs and Aura City. It seemed like a good place to arrange such a meeting. As agreed, Dac showed up alone. Quentin and Emmaline reluctantly stayed in Aura City. Jace assured Dac that all was set in place. The plan had been for Quentin to go to Alex pretending he had double crossed Dac and made his own deal Jace. He would give Alex a name to give to Jace. Dac would give Emmaline the name of Cloe's killer, instructing her to go to Luca and give this name to Jace in exchange for Nikolai's location. Emmaline was to tell Luca she had figured it out and was giving the information to him so that Dac would forgive Harper and she could come home. Luca was so desperate to repair his relationship with his brother that he would never expect the setup. Dac, of course, never revealing his true intentions, would arrive first to meet up location. Alex would show up, expecting to find the dead bodies of both Dac and Nikolai. Instead, he would find only Dac, who was very much alive. Jace would make sure Luca and Harper arrived with Nikolai at least an hour after Alex. Although if Dac knew his brother, Luca would send Harper away before meeting with Dac in an attempt to keep her safe. In fact, Dac was counting on Luca to do exactly that. This would give Dac time to take out Alex before Luca or Nikolai could interfere. Given Luca's history with Alex, neither Dac nor Jace was willing to trust he would allow Alex to be killed, and Nikolai definitely would never allow the murder of his son. So, they had it carefully planned out. Jace would meet Luca and Harper to hand over Nikolai, and by the time they arrived at the meeting spot with Dac, Alex would already be dead.

Dac sat on the ledge of the exposed second floor, his back against the wall, one leg stretched out in front of him, the other dangling from the edge. He felt surprisingly calm and confident. He stared up at the sky through the spaces where the ceiling had caved in. Patiently he waited for the arrival of Alex. The hunger inside him was starting to creep up since he had not drunk anything since the night before. But he needed that hunger to do what he had planned for tonight. The sensation of needing blood fueling the vampiric instincts he had tried so desperately to suppress. On this night, however, those instincts would be the very thing to set him free from himself and allow him to become what he should have been all this time.

He stayed quiet as Alex finally appeared through the entryway. Carefully he brought his leg back up on the ledge. Keeping against the wall, he hugged his knees as he silently watched Alex search the room. Alex called out, and his voice echoed off the bare walls. Dac watched Alex as he walked from room to room on the first floor of this old house, unaware of Dac's presence. Each time he called out for Jace, the anger in Alex's voice grew more intense. Still, Dac waited for the perfect moment to reveal himself or not. He wanted to take him by surprise. He sat up there, hidden by the darkness watching and waiting, and just when Alex began to head for the stairs, he stood. Alex had one foot on the bottom step when Dac descended upon him. Dac grabbed Alex from behind, one arm around his throat, the other around his chest. Alex struggled under his grasp. Dac held him tight. He sunk his teeth into the vampire's neck, draining him of the blood keeping him alive. Once he got his fill, he tossed the weakened vampire to the ground.

Alex stared up at Dac, stunned. "You were supposed to be dead," Alex said to him. His voice was weak, but it vibrated with rage. Dac kicked him in the stomach. Alex coughed and clutched his stomach as he feebly tried to peel himself off the floor. Dac pushed him back to the ground. He stood over him. His boot pressing into the other vampire's chest, he shifted his weight, leaning in towards Alex. He rested his arms on his thigh, then said, "I know exactly what you were planning. Did you really think I would allow you to take what is mine? I'm guessing not since you wanted me killed."

Alex wheezed as he tried to take a breath, "It's not like you wanted it anyway, or you would have taken it a long time ago." Even in his weakened state, he stayed defiant.

"What I want or don't want is none of your concern, nor does that give you any right to it." Dac pressed his foot harder into Alex's chest, causing him to cough as he gasped for air. He struggled under

Dac's weight, trying to get free. Dac laughed at Alex's poor attempts to free himself. He pulled a flask from his back pocket. Inside contained the oils poisonous to their kind. He unscrewed the lid to the flask. With one hand, he grabbed Alex by the jaw, squeezing the muscles and forcing his mouth to open. With the other hand that held onto the flask, Dac poured the poisonous contents down Alex's throat.

Dac removed his foot from Alex's chest. He stood back and watched with sick pleasure as the vampire convulsed on the ground as the poison made its way through his system. Once Alex stopped shaking, and his body finally lay still, Dac stood back over the enemy vampire. He took the knife from his other pocket. He removed the casing that covered the blade. With a firm grip on the handle, he plunged the knife into Alex's chest. Dac withdrew the knife. He watched the remaining blood which he hadn't drank earlier pour out from the wound, then hauled Alex's lifeless body away. He grabbed Alex by the ankles and dragged him across the floor, leaving a trail of dirt, dust, and blood along the way. He stuffed the body inside a hall closet and went back to the main foyer to await the arrival of his brother and his old friends. With Alex now out of the way, Nikolai would now be safe, and Dac could take back from his brother what was rightfully his.

Dac was sitting on the stairs inside the old house. His elbows rested on his knees, and his chin rested on folded hands. He was staring straight ahead at nothingness when Luca finally entered. Luca was alone, however. Neither Harper nor Nikolai accompanied him. As expected, Luca must have told Harper to stay away. Dac was, however, a little disappointed Nikolai had not shown. They had once hunted down his brother together, and Dac would have loved to have Nikolai at his side once again. He had hoped for Nikolai's forgiveness but wasn't surprised his old friend still needed more time. It did not occur to him that Jace would renege on this end of the agreement and not set Nikolai free. And even he had, Jace already told Dac where Nikolai was being kept. As much as he would have liked Nikolai at this side, the fact that he wasn't there would not deter Dac from his plans.

The warm breeze from overhead began to stir the dirt and dust that covered the exposed interior of the old, abandoned house. Luca's steps echoed as he crossed the worn tiled floor. Dac sat still on the stairs. The knife in his hand still dripped with Alex's blood. The moonlight reflected off its blade. Red flickered in the pupils of Luca's eyes, indicating the demon inside him was very present. Dac flashed his fanged teeth. Luca stood in front of his brother, holding his stare.

"Where is Nikolai?" Dac finally asked, breaking the silence between them.

"He's safe." He lied, unsure whether Nikolai was in truth safe or not.

"And Harper?"

"She is safe too." Luca glanced down at the bloody knife. "And Alex?"

"He won't be a problem any longer."

"I see." Luca took a few steps back. His eyes still glowing with red.

"He not only wanted me and Nikolai dead, but he wanted you dead also. He wanted the demon inside you. He wanted your power. I wasn't about to let that happen." Dac explained, noticing Luca's gaze fixated on the knife in his hand.

"So, you saved my life? Is that what you're saying?"

Dac set the knife on the ground, ignoring Luca's question. He stood up from his seat on the steps and walked over to stand face to face with his brother. "So, you've come alone? What do you want?"

Luca put his hand on Dac's shoulder. "The same thing I've always wanted, to be your brother. Yet somehow, we always seem to be on opposite sides. I want to end this constant tension between us. I want to understand your hatred for me and find a way to end it."

"You know, I think you're right. We should end this tension between us. Let's be brothers like we should have been all along." Dac

216

noticed the red glow fading from Luca's eyes as he said these words. He was letting his guard down. Dac smiled at his brother, hiding his fangs to show he was sincere. "Come, let's go someplace we can sit and talk."

He led Luca to another room. Dirty linens covered the furniture that had been left behind when the house's last occupants had moved away. Dac removed two of the dirt-covered white sheets to reveal a couple of wingback chairs. He gestured to Luca to sit in one, and he sat in the other.

Together they sat in the dark mucky room. They talked about the past. Dac expressed his disdain for his vampiric instincts and how he had blamed his brother for turning him into a monster before he had only recently learned of the curse. Luca apologized for the way he had done things all those years ago, and Dac apologized for his past transgressions.

"But there's one thing I need to know," Dac said before asking, "why did you do it? Why did you consume the demon yourself? Could you not have just killed him and been done with it, ended the curse?"

"I wish I could have, but no. I couldn't end the curse without killing you, and I was not going to do that. I took the demon so that you would not turn evil. So that you could retain as much of your innocence as possible. But I had to turn you before the curse did. Everything I had done was to save your life."

"I believe you. I forgive you." Dac stood up, and Luca followed. Dac reached out to his brother, embracing him in a hug. While holding him tight in his brotherly embrace, he snatched the knife he had known Luca would have hidden at his side. With the knife clutched firmly in his hand, he thrust it into the center of his brother's chest.

Dac stepped away from his brother. Luca's eyes were full of shock, pain, and despair, but his mouth released no sound as it filled with blood. Still holding the handle of the knife, Dac yanked it out from Luca's chest with great force. The red glow from the demon flashed momentarily in his eyes and then quickly faded away. Luca's body fell to the ground. Dac stared at the knife in his hand. Blood dripped from the knife to the floor. The red substance covered his hand and pooled around his feet. The drumming sound of a heartbeat surrounded the room. He kept his eyes fixated on the the knife. At the edge of the blade was the heart of the demon.

Finally, it was his, his legacy and birthright. He let the knife drop to the ground. He held the heart cupped in his hands. He brought his hands to his mouth, and like his brother had done four centuries before him, he devoured the demon into himself. Inside him, he could feel the heart of the demon uniting with his own. The demon's blood raced through his veins, fueling his body with its power. All of his nerves tingled with electricity. It was done. He was now the vampire he was always meant to be.

The sound of voices and footsteps echoed from the other room. One of those voices he recognized belonged to Nikolai. The other was the voice of an unfamiliar female. Dac turned towards the doorway as the footsteps grew closer. Nikolai appeared on the other side of the entryway. A dark-haired vampire stood at his side. It was Una. Dac smiled at the irony.

"What have you done?" Nikolai demanded, seeing Dac's blood-stained face and clothes. His eyes shifted to the body of Luca lying on the ground. The gaping hole in his chest gave away the answer without Dac needing to say a word. Dac could sense Nikolai's disapproval, but he no longer cared. He felt a heat building behind his eyes as he stared past his old friend. The large black wings extended from his back, and he lept off the ground ascending through the fallen ceiling of the old house and into the warm night sky.

Thirty-One

Harper stood in front of the Aura City train station. She looked behind her one last time. Luca had already gone, though she could still feel his presence surrounding her. Over the past few weeks, he had become her friend and protector. Although she knew protecting her was exactly what he was doing now, it still hurt her heart a little to leave him behind to deal with Alex and then Dac alone.

She walked up the steps to the station platform. There she purchased her ticket to Noxwood. She picked up a schedule from the stack on the wall and pretended to read it while she waited for the train to arrive. It was not long before she heard the whistle of the train and its tires screeching across the tracks. She got in line alongside the other passengers and boarded the train handing her ticket over to the conductor.

Sitting on the train, Harper watched as the summer rain dripped steadily from the darkened sky. The water splashed up from the tracks as the train sped along. She checked the time on the cell phone she carried with her. She should reach Noxwood about an hour before sunrise.

The pit of her stomach ached with the worry of what might be happening in Aura City. When they had received the call from Jace that the meeting with Alex was finally set, Luca insisted Harper leave town and go to his house in Noxwood. Lizbeth and Sonya would be expecting her.

The last time she was at that house, she was a prisoner. The thought of that experience sent shivers down her spine. Memories of being chained to the wall, watching Una stab Nikolai, and Nikolai falling lifelessly to the ground flooded her mind. Tears formed in the corner of her eyes. She wiped them away. Never would she have thought she would be going there now voluntarily. Nor would she have ever thought Luca would have turned out to be the good guy. It turned out Alex had been pulling all the strings the entire time, but after tonight, all that was going to end.

Luca promised her before she left for the train station that he would take care of things with Alex. Luca had been reluctant to harm Alex since Alex was the one who had saved his life all those years ago, but he finally came to realize that Alex was out of control. He needed to be stopped. Once Alex was dealt with, Luca promised to repair his relationship with Dac so that Harper could go home. Although the home she had shared with Dac, Nikolai, and the others no longer felt like her home. She was not even sure now that she wanted to return. Maybe she would remain in Noxwood with Luca. She would tell him when he arrived there the next day as he promised he would.

The train arrived at their first station stop. Harper looked down at her phone again, then looked at the schedule she had picked up at the station before she boarded the train. They were making good time. People began boarding the train. Harper pulled her hair in front of her face and continued staring out the window. She kept her bag on the seat next to her, hoping to deter anyone from sitting next to her. The new travelers walked down the aisle of the train car, some stopping to put their luggage on the overhead racks and take a seat. Others continued moving into other cars. Harper breathed a quiet sigh of relief when the train began moving again. There were only two other stops before reaching her destination in Noxwood. Thank God for express trains, Harper thought to herself.

The trip to Noxwood was long. When the train finally reached the station, Harper stood up and stretched her muscles. She grabbed her bag and hurried off the train onto the station platform. The first time she had been to Luca's house here in Noxood, she had traveled in the confines of a coffin and therefore had no idea how to get there or any way to gauge the distance from the station to the house. She looked around and spotted a taxi at the edge of the parking lot. It appeared to be empty except for the driver. She leaned into the opened passenger window and asked him if he could take her to her destination. When he nodded yes, she hopped in the back seat of the cab and gave the man the address to Luca's house. Along the way, she chatted to the driver the way Luca had taught her, making him comfortable and gaining his confidence that she was a safe passenger. When they rolled up near Luca's house, she instructed the driver to park a few feet past the front gate under the canopy of a lush green tree. She handed him cash for the ride. As he counted the money in his hand, Harper reached forward, placing one hand around the man's chest and the other across his mouth. She could feel him trying to struggle under the weight of her grasp, but her vampiric strength and the seatbelt he wore for safety restricted his movements. Harper leaned in, placing her mouth on the side of the man's throat, and sunk her fangs into his flesh.

Harper stood outside the large iron gates. She glared up at the house Luca called his home, seeing it for the first time in all its glory. The castle-like façade stood tall against the mountainous backdrop. As she passed through the unlocked gates making her way to the house, she let her fingertips graze the cement of the two-tiered fountain that stood in the center of the stone walkway. The water cascading down the fountain splashed onto her hand. She stood admiring it only for a moment. The night sky was becoming a lighter shade of blue, with sunrise vastly approaching. Her vampiric senses were beginning to grow weaker. It was only a matter of time before she would need to seek the safety of pure darkness.

She took the steps one at a time to the front door. When no one answered her knocks, she reached for the handle. The door was unlocked, and she stepped carefully inside. She called out to Lizbeth and Sonya. The only sound she heard was that of her own voice echoing through the empty halls. Maybe they had already gone to sleep, she thought to herself. Only something did not feel quite right. Luca had assured her they would be expecting her. Why would they not await her arrival, knowing that she would not know her way around the house? She called out for them again. Still, only silence and echoes answered.

Harper stepped away from the foyer in search of her two hostesses. She turned into the familiar front parlor room. One of the only few rooms she had seen as a prisoner here less than a year ago. It felt strange to now be here of her own free will. As she stepped inside the room, she gasped at the gruesome sight that beheld her. Splatters of red covered every surface from floor to ceiling. Blood smeared the walls, and the pool of deep crimson at her feet flowed from the headless body of a dead vampire. Wanting to get out of there as fast as she could, she turned to leave the room only to find Jace standing in the entryway.

"What did you do?" Her voice shook as she felt the words escape from her lips. She had never feared her friend until this very moment. Jace stepped further into the room. His movements were slow as he crept closer to her. The dagger he held in his hand dripping with blood was pointed at her, the very same dagger she had given to him not so long ago.

"I was told I would find Cloe's killers here." He answered. "I was told I know her when I saw her. Never in a million years would I have guessed it could be you, but now here we are, face to face." There were tears struggling to break free from the ducts of his eyes. His face was full of anguish and disgust.

Harper tried to speak, but the words would not form this time. Her time had come. She would not try and fight him, she decided. He deserved his justice. Cloe deserved justice.

Jace was standing close to her now. She could smell the blood pulsing in his veins and the blood on the knife, and blood all around the room. She could hear his heart beating steady and fast. She reached out to him touching her palm to his face. "I'm sorry," was all she could manage to say as he thrust the dagger deep into the center of her chest.

JACE HELD A FIRM GRIP on the leather-bound handle of the dagger. The blade lodged in Harper's chest. He couldn't bring himself to remove it. Her eyes clouded over. The words "I'm sorry" barely escaped her lips in a whisper. The hand she held to his face slid down to her side. Her mouth gaped open as the blood poured from the wound in her chest. She coughed and wheezed as she struggled to take a breath. He did not want to believe it was her, but as soon as he saw her, he knew. The guilt read like an open book on her face. And now he stood in front of her with her life in his hands. Her mind was open to him.

The dark-haired vampire coming closer to her as she screamed in shock and disbelief. "Harper, no! What are you doing? Harper, wait!" Cloe had screamed that first night. Harper's glistening white fanged teeth dug into Cloe's throat, tasting her blood. She would come back night after night, stealing moments when Cloe was alone, siphoning more and more of her blood until that day, Cloe fainted, and Jace rushed her to the hospital. Cloe had stayed in the hospital for weeks, and Jace had suspected a vampire but could never find the marks. Then one day, Cloe seemed to recover from her strange illness. Jace took her home, and that's when Harper appeared to her one last time.

That last fateful evening, Harper came to her friend's apartment and appeared in her bedroom. She was alone for the first time since her hospital stay. Harper brushed the curls away from Cloe's face as she lay resting. She gently turned Cloe's head away from her. She lifted her hair, exposing her neck. She leaned in close and whispered something in Cloe's ear. And then she took her last bite. A short time later, Cloe had awoken. She took her life that night, slitting her wrists while she lay in the bathtub. Jace blamed himself for not getting there earlier. But now, he only blamed one. The one who called herself his best friend. The one who had once been Cloe's best friend. The dark-haired vampire standing before him now with the blade of the dagger in her chest, dying.

Jace turned his gaze away from the vampire's eyes. Sarah was standing behind her. The ax raised over her shoulder. Jace took a step back. The dagger still in his hand slid out from where it was lodged in Harper's chest, leaving a gaping open wound. The blood poured out faster. Sarah swung the ax. The sharp blade of the ax cut through Harper's neck. Blood splattered across Sarah's face, shirt, and hands. Harper's body dropped to the floor. Her severed head fell to the ground, rolling mere inches away.

"Our work here is done," Sarah said. She wiped her face with a towel she removed from the back pocket of her black pants. With the ax still in her hand, she walked past Jace into the foyer and out the front door.

Jace took one last look back at the massacre behind him. Though he was not a religious man, he whispered a short prayer for Harper. And another one for Cloe. He followed Sarah out of this house of horrors. Justice was now served.

Acknowledgments

I'd like to say thank you to all my family and friends for all of your love and support following me on this writing journey. I know I can probably be annoying babbling on about my books and asking all my weird questions so thank you for putting up with me. Thank you to Elisa Pinto and Jennifer Lesperance for reading my very raw 1st chapters and rough draft and helping me work through the places I got stuck and for asking the important questions. Thank you to Lynn for pointing out all the typos I missed in the 1st book so I could fix them and also for your critique, even if you did take a whole year to read it. Your honestly is priceless. Sorry, I can't promise no more cliffhangers. Lol. To Gina Maglione-Piacenza, thank you for the constant pics you sent until I found the perfect one for the backdrop of my cover, even if I did manipulate it a bit. Speaking of the cover, thanks to all in the family group chats, your honest opinions truly helped to make it better. I fully appreciate it. To my godmother, Anne Marie Mcguigan, I have a story in the works just for you. ☺

Also by Ana DiPinto

Scorned in Blood Trilogy
Scorned in Blood
Scorned In Darkness

www.ingramcontent.com/pod-product-compliance
Lightning Source LLC
Chambersburg PA
CBHW022013170626
46808CB00001B/386